Dawn Demons

Dawn Demons

by

Peter J Murray

First published in Great Britain by Mokee Joe Promotions in 2007

A Catalogue record for this book is available from the British Library

ISBN-10: 0 955 34155 8
ISBN-13: 978 0995 34155 7

Typeset in Perpetua by Avon DataSet Ltd, Bidford on Avon, Warwickshire

Printed in the UK by CPI Bookmarque, Croydon, CR0 4TD

The paper and board used in this paperback by Mokee Joe Promotions are natural recyclable products made from wood grown in sustainable forests. The manufacturing processes conform to the environmental regulations of the country of origin.

Mokee Joe Promotions
Riverside
8 Rivock Avenue
Steeton
BD20 6SA

www.peterjmurray.co.uk

Contents

Scullion

Prologue

Little, wooden, fleshy face
Full of evil, full of grace
Is he good or is he bad?
Spooky little sailor lad

PJM

Red sky at night . . . shepherds' delight.
Red sky dawning . . . sailors' warning.

ANON

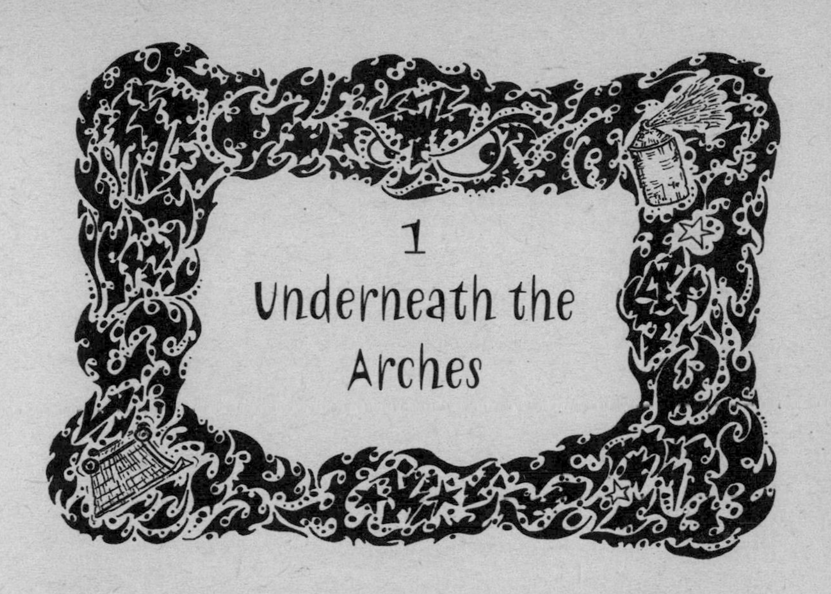

1 Underneath the Arches

The train emerged slowly from the tunnel, rattling and bumping along the tracks. The station platform was only minutes away.

Calum stared in fascination out of the window. 'Wow! Look at those old archways. They look really creepy. I wonder what they were used for?'

Billy looked out at the crumbling Victorian brickwork and shook his head. 'I've no idea. Look . . . there's an arch with a door.'

Calum nodded.

The train passed under a bridge and moved closer to the embankment. Billy frowned at the jumble of litter strewn along the edge of the rails: bottles, cans . . . even an old mattress. As they passed under another road-bridge, more archways appeared, and then the most striking graffiti painted on the brickwork.

'Wow!' Calum gasped. 'Some artist!'

Billy, who had always enjoyed art, stared at the bold style and vivid colouring of the lettering. He nodded enthusiastically.

A voice sounded over the intercom: '*The next station is Scawlsby on Sea. The train will terminate here. Please check you have all your belongings.*'

Billy's mind wandered to the cosy Victorian house at number ten, Gladstone Terrace. Aunt Emily had invited him and Calum to stay for a few days. Scawlsby on Sea was definitely not the most picturesque of towns, especially during the winter. But it was still a seaside place, and with Calum – his best friend – alongside him, he just knew that they were going to have a great time.

The train slowed, bumped and jolted its way along the jumble of tracks. The boys stood up and reached for their bags.

'Come on, Mum! We're here!' Billy said excitedly.

Mrs Hardacre had been dozing for the last half hour. Billy's two-year-old sister, Beth, had slept soundly by her side. Mrs Hardacre stretched and yawned. 'Are you boys OK with those bags?'

'No problem, Mrs H!' Calum replied.

Billy manhandled the bigger of the bags towards the end of the carriage. 'We'll wait by the door, Mum,' he said.

The train passed under the shadow of another road-bridge and ground to a halt. Billy put his bag down on the floor and stood with his legs astride it. The carriage was only a metre away from the underside of the bridge. He found himself staring through the window at an image daubed in bright paint directly in front of him.

'Hey, Calum! Look at this!'

The graffiti depicted what looked like a wheely bin, but with the lid lifted slightly. Sinister eyes stared out from the shadow just beneath it. The word 'SCULLION' was painted in dramatic style down the side of the bin.

The image fascinated and disturbed Billy at the same time. The eyes peering out from below the lid – they looked really menacing . . . almost threatening.

The train lurched forward again.

'That's weird!' Calum exclaimed. 'And look . . . there's more of them.'

Both boys watched spellbound as the image repeated itself along the crumbling brickwork of the station approach . . . at least ten more wheely bins . . . ten more sets of evil eyes staring out from below the lids . . . the word 'SCULLION' running diagonally across each bin.

The train finally pulled up alongside the platform.

Billy pushed the button by the side of the door. It hissed open.

A few moments later, he and Calum had the bags on

the platform. They waited patiently whilst Mrs Hardacre took Beth away to make a 'loo stop'.

'Who do you think painted that graffiti?'

Calum shook his head. 'I've no idea.'

Billy's mum reappeared with Beth in her arms. 'OK you two? Let's go and find a taxi.'

Billy and Calum picked up their bags. Mrs Hardacre put Beth down and grabbed her overnight bag. They made their way up the platform and passed into the main station. As they moved through the station exit and out into the street, a group of people brushed by them on their way in. Billy suddenly felt compelled to look over his shoulder. A girl, about the same age as himself, turned and stared back. She smiled and he quickly looked away, the colour rushing into his cheeks. But her face was 'freeze-framed' in his mind . . . a pale, smiling face with shiny white teeth and clear determined eyes. His arms began to ache. He walked on a few paces, stopped and put his bag down on the floor. He took a deep breath and looked back. She was gone!

'Are you OK, Billy?' Calum asked. 'What are you staring at?'

'There was a girl . . .' Billy whispered. 'She was staring at me.'

'Oh yeah!' Calum chuckled. 'In your dreams!'

'I'm telling you –'

'Come on, you two!' Billy's mum called to them.

'Let's get to Emily's! I'm gasping for a cup of tea.'

They moved out into the street. It was beginning to get dark and the cracked paving slabs glistened in the drizzle. Billy shivered a little and felt a tinge of excitement as he recalled the girl's face. Why had she smiled at him? It was almost as if she'd recognized him.

'Come on, Billy! Stop daydreaming!' Calum teased, as he climbed into the taxi.

A few seconds later, they were being driven along streets lined with brightly-coloured Victorian houses. But Billy noticed lots of vandalism . . . bus shelters with broken windows, upturned supermarket trolleys littering shop fronts, and graffiti daubed across almost every available wall space.

No one in the taxi spoke. Even Beth remained silent. The extensive vandalism and the drizzly weather combined to blot out the colourful nature of the old seaside town.

Billy's mum finally broke the silence. 'Almost there!' she said in a cheery voice. 'I hope your Aunt Emily's got the kettle on.'

The taxi turned into Gladstone Terrace.

'By the way,' Mrs Hardacre said with a slightly nervous edge to her voice, 'Aunt Emily's taken in a lodger. His name's Henry Prior. He's an old man. Apparently he's a bit grumpy, but Emily says he's harmless enough and won't bother you.'

Billy looked at Calum and Calum stared back.

'Why does she need a lodger, Mum?' Billy asked, sensing his mother wasn't over-pleased with the idea.

Mrs Hardacre sighed. 'It all helps to pay the bills. Her part-time job pays precious little, and ever since Uncle Jack died . . .'

As the taxi finally drew up outside number ten, the wind whipped up and the drizzle turned to driving rain. Aunt Emily appeared at the door and shouted at them to get inside. Though she was smiling, Billy saw the worry in her eyes. And then he saw that her front garden was strewn with litter . . . bottles, cans and all manner of rubbish.

'Hi Em! What's happened here?' Billy's mum shouted through the rain. She trotted up the path with Beth clinging tightly to her.

'I'll tell you when you're all inside,' Aunt Emily shouted back. 'Hurry up, Billy . . . and – Calum, isn't it? Come on in . . . out of the rain.'

Billy picked up his bag and pushed open the gate. As he set off up the path, he failed to see the face peering down from the bedroom window. It was an old man's face, wrinkled and grey. It stared at Billy with sad eyes . . . a haunting expression . . . finally disappearing back behind the lace curtains.

2
Aunt Emily's

Aunt Emily greeted each of them in turn. She embraced Billy's mum, moved on to Beth, gave Billy a hug, and finished by shaking Calum's hand. Although Aunt Emily was only a few years older than his mum, her face looked much older . . . *more wrinkled than the last time*, Billy thought to himself.

She brushed a hand over her greying head and led them through the hallway into the sitting room. A big fire roared in the hearth. The warmth of the dancing flames made Billy feel calmer and more relaxed.

'So how are you, Em?' Mrs Hardacre asked, taking a cigarette from her bag.

Auntie Emily said nothing. She frowned at the cigarette. Billy watched as his mum put it back in the packet. 'Sorry! Force of habit . . . I'll smoke it outside later.'

'It's such a bad habit, Pauline. I can't understand why you don't give it up.'

'Easier said than done,' Billy's mum replied. 'Anyway . . . that's *my* problem. What happened to the garden?'

Billy looked straight at Aunt Emily, wondering what she would say. Her garden had always been the best-kept in the street. She took a real pride in it.

'I'll tell you later,' was all she said.

While Aunt Emily went off and busied herself in the kitchen, Billy's mum hung their coats up and the two boys made themselves comfortable

Billy scanned around at the old-fashioned décor of the room . . . bright flowered wallpaper, chintz curtains and a strikingly bold patterned carpet covered in red and orange swirls.

'This house is really cosy,' Calum said. 'Who's that man in the photograph?'

Billy followed Calum's gaze up to the mantelpiece above the fire.

'That was Billy's Uncle Jack,' Mrs Hardacre replied. 'He died ten years ago. He was a good man.'

Billy went over to the photograph, picked it up and gazed at Uncle Jack's striking features. Jet-black curly hair topped his bronzed face. His warm smile revealed rows of flashing white teeth (Aunt Emily said that Uncle Jack was always smiling.) The eyes were steely blue – so clear and full of life.

He passed the photograph to Calum. 'He was a member of the lifeboat crew,' Billy said proudly. 'He saved loads of lives.'

'One hundred and three to be exact,' Aunt Emily chipped in, placing a tray of scones down on the coffee table. 'He'd worked with the fishing fleet and been a voluntary member of the Scawlsby Lifeboat Crew for seventeen years, ever since he'd left school.'

'That's fantastic!' Calum said, eyeing the scones at the same time.

'He loved the sea, and that's what killed him in the end.'

A hush fell across the room. The fire crackled and hissed.

'There was a great storm and a shipwreck,' Billy's mum said sadly. 'Lots of men lost their lives that night.'

'Enough of that,' Aunt Emily said, forcing a smile. 'Help yourselves to scones and jam while I go and get the drinks.

The rain continued to splatter on the windows and the wind whistled down the chimney making the flames dance brightly. It was good to be tucked up inside. And yet Billy sensed that all was far from cosy in his aunt's little terraced house.

He bit into a fresh scone smothered in raspberry jam . . . it tasted good and he cheered up. He cheered up even more as Beth licked at her scone and covered her face in jam and cream. Calum said she looked like a little clown who'd just been hit in the face with a custard pie, and this made Billy laugh.

And then something made Billy look over his shoulder towards the door . . . and his heart skipped a beat.

An old man's face peered around the door at them – sad eyes . . . staring . . . penetrating – and then it was gone.

Aunt Emily clutched her mug of tea and spoke in a shaky voice. 'Vandals! They did it. They're a damn nuisance! I didn't hear a thing. I just got up this morning and there it was. Litter and rubbish everywhere. It's senseless!'

'Em, that's really bad . . . I know how much you love your garden,' Billy's mum said sympathetically.

Aunt Emily took a sip of tea before continuing. 'We *all* love our gardens – or at least we did! Now folks are starting to give up. And you can't blame them. What's the point? They just trash everything.'

'Has anyone been in touch with the police?' Billy's mum asked.

'Yes . . . we all have.'

'And . . .?' she asked expectantly.

'Nothing!' Aunt Emily sighed. 'The police say they're keeping a look out. But nobody's ever caught. The whole town's rife with it . . . there's vandalism everywhere. It's killing the place.'

Billy looked across to his friend. Calum read his thoughts. 'Billy Hardacre, private investigator . . . he'll get to the bottom of it,' Calum quipped.

Aunt Emily frowned. 'From what I've heard, you two had more than enough adventures on your last holiday. I'm sure the police will get to the bottom of it, and in the meantime, you can enjoy yourselves and keep out of trouble. The forecast's not too bad for the next few days.'

'I think I'd better go and get this little madam cleaned up and ready for bed,' Billy's mum said, smiling. She picked Beth up and moved towards the door.

'Watch out for Henry!' Aunt Emily said. 'He's harmless enough, but he creeps about the place.'

'Your new lodger,' Billy said. 'Mum told us.'

'Yes, he was a friend of your grandad. He's had a lot of bad luck recently and he needed somewhere to stay.'

'What sort of bad luck?' Calum asked.

Both boys watched as Aunt Emily took another sip of tea. 'Well, a few weeks ago his kitchen caught fire and half his house burnt down.'

'Wow . . . that really is bad luck,' Billy sighed. 'How did it happen?'

'Says he left a pan on . . . silly old duffer!' Aunt Emily said. 'Fire brigade got there just in time. He was upstairs. They had to get him down on one of their ladders.'

Billy looked back towards the door of the living room.

There was a dark space between the edge of the door and the hallway. He half expected to see the old man's eyes peering through again . . . but there was no one.

That night, Billy tossed and turned on the bed settee. Aunt Emily had set it up in the sitting room. The fire had died down, but it was still throwing out some heat. Perhaps the room was too warm. Perhaps his mind was too active. Perhaps it was Calum snoring loudly by his side. Whatever the reason, Billy found himself unable to get to sleep.

When he finally did drop off, he dreamt he was walking underwater . . . on the seabed . . . weaving in and out of great fronds of seaweed . . . looking for something, but he didn't know what. And then, in the distance, through a wavering blue haze, he saw a shoal of big fish. And as he moved closer, he saw that they were dolphins . . . all swimming in a circle . . . around something . . . the same something he knew he was looking for.

As he moved closer still, the dolphins parted to reveal a mermaid sitting at their centre . . . a beautiful young mermaid with long blonde hair and a familiar face. She stared at him, her clear green eyes intense and penetrating . . . delving into his mind.

Billy woke up in a cold sweat, desperately trying to think where he'd seen that face. And then – as consciousness fully returned – he knew!

He rolled over to face Calum and whispered loudly. 'Calum! Wake up. You won't believe this!'

'Calum stopped snoring, grunted and half opened his eyes. "What are you on about?"

'The girl . . . the one that smiled at me in the railway station . . .'

'Yeah . . . like I said before . . . in your dreams!'

Billy pushed himself up on to his elbows and stared at Calum with wide eyes. 'That's exactly the point,' he whispered excitedly. 'I've just seen her again . . . *in my dreams*!'

3
Beside the Seaside

Billy and Calum walked quietly up to the kitchen table. The old man sat at one end; Billy's mum sat at the other, Beth by her side.

'Here they are! Morning, boys! Come on . . . sit yourselves down,' Aunt Emily said, smiling at them. 'Now this is Henry – my lodger.'

Billy sat down and glanced across at Henry. He was eating a bowl of cereal. He raised his eyes and nodded his head ever so slightly.

'Henry . . . this is Billy – my nephew – and his friend, Calum. They're staying with me for a few days during half term. My sister's leaving them with me.'

Henry raised his eyes again, looked Billy and Calum up and down, and went back to his cereal.

The boys cast a glance at each other and concentrated

their attention on Billy's mum and Beth – it was much easier!

'What time are you going home, Mum?' Billy asked.

'I'm going into town with Emily – on her way to work – and then I'll be off. Don't worry, you'll soon be rid of us!' Mrs Hardacre said with a smile.

Helping themselves to cereal and toast, the boys talked quietly and made plans for the day. Henry finished his cereal, slurped his mug of tea – rather too loudly, Billy thought to himself – and left without speaking.

'You'll soon get used to old Henry,' Aunt Emily said, pouring herself a cup of tea. 'He's a heart of gold underneath that grumpy exterior. And he's had a lot to put up with one way or another.'

Billy nodded. It wasn't every day that someone's house half burnt down.

'It's a lovely day today, boys,' Aunt Emily said from the sink. She was already washing some of the breakfast dishes and gazing out of the window. The sunlight streamed in and lit up the kitchen.

Billy suddenly remembered the rubbish strewn across her garden. 'Have you got any bin liners? We could clear the garden for you.'

'Bless!' she said, smiling towards her sister. 'You've a good lad there, Pauline.'

'You don't have to tell me,' Billy's mum replied proudly. 'And Calum . . . he's not so bad either.'

Calum took a bite from his slice of toast and pretended not to hear.

Breakfast finished, both boys left the table and headed off towards the garden. They each had two black bin liners supplied by Aunt Emily from the cupboard under the kitchen sink. Billy was eager to get started.

Calum wasn't quite so enthusiastic. 'Why did you have to go and say that? Great start to the holiday – picking up rubbish! We'll probably pick up a disease and finish up in hospital!'

'I just felt sorry for her,' Billy said quietly. 'I wanted to cheer her up.'

Calum sighed. 'OK! It shouldn't take us too long if we get stuck in.'

Whilst Calum watched, Billy tore one of the bin liners into two and wrapped the black plastic around his right hand. Calum did the same. A few minutes later they were out in the morning sunshine, picking up the rubbish with their protected hand and dropping it into a bin liner held in the other.

As Calum had predicted, it didn't take long. After a final search amongst Aunt Emily's shrubs and bushes, Calum found something interesting.

'What do you make of this?' he shouted, holding up a small round object. He dropped it on to the garden path.

Billy walked over and peered down at it. 'It looks like a little hat.' He picked it up and examined it more closely, his hand still wrapped in the bin liner. It was white with a black band around it. A small emblem stood out on the front of it. 'Look at this. It looks like a small anchor.'

Calum stood with his hands on his hips and stared at it, deep in thought. 'I've got it!' he said triumphantly. 'It's a doll's hat . . . a sailor doll!'

Billy looked at Calum admiringly. Calum was brainy. And what with Billy being practical . . . they made a good team.

Billy stuffed the little cap in his pocket. He decided to ask Aunt Emily about it later. He did a final sweep through the garden, tied each bag of rubbish securely and placed them in the wheely bin round the back of the house.

Aunt Emily was more than pleased to have her garden neat and tidy again. Even the late-flowering shrubs seemed to glow with pride in the autumn sunshine. She gave Billy and Calum some money to treat themselves down on the promenade. The sailor cap remained in Billy's pocket . . . He forgot all about it.

By mid-morning, the sky had turned cloudy. A cold wind whistled up the cobbled street, but at least it wasn't raining. As the two friends walked side by side, heading towards the seafront, Billy glanced to his left down an alleyway and saw an abandoned shopping trolley lying on its side, empty lager cans scattered around it. There was graffiti daubed across a redbrick wall, but nothing like the spectacular artwork they'd seen by the rail tracks.

He turned back to Calum. 'That girl I saw at the station – the one I dreamt about – I can't stop thinking about her.'

'You've got it bad, Billy-boy!' Calum replied, looking eagerly towards the seafront. 'Maybe you need a girlfriend.' He sniffed the air and ran on ahead. 'Come on . . . I can smell candyfloss.'

Despite the cold autumn day, most of the amusements and food stalls were open for half term. A wooden shack adorned with the word 'CANDYFLOSS' in faded painted letters caught their attention. They each bought a stick and continued on towards an amusement arcade.

'Look!' Calum suddenly cried out. 'They've got Zombie Attack!'

They shuffled up behind the huge computer screen and watched in fascination as the player concentrated on destroying a line of zombies.

'Wow! He's doing really well,' Calum almost shouted from the back of the seated figure.

A zombie, scarier than the rest, suddenly appeared on the screen and hurled a missile towards the player. The screen exploded in a blaze of colour and then the words 'GAME OVER' appeared.

The boy swivelled round to face Billy and Calum. He

was wearing a red baseball cap and his face looked even redder. 'You dorks! You broke my concentration!'

Billy took a step backwards. Calum did the same. 'Sorry!' Calum said meekly. 'I didn't mean to . . . I thought you were doing really well.'

The boy stood up. He was tall . . . at least a foot taller than Calum. 'That's just the point, mate . . . I *was* doing well – until you two geeks turned up.'

Billy and Calum took another step backwards.

At the same time, four more boys appeared. They wore similar red baseball caps and none of them smiled. One of the four was bigger than the rest. He wore gold rings on all his fingers and a small ring through his top lip. 'You owe Kez some money,' he said in a gruff voice.

'W-why . . .?' Calum stammered.

'You made him lose . . . so it only seems right that you pay up . . . so that he can play again.'

The other boys scowled and nodded in agreement.

Billy glanced sideways at Calum. Calum read his thoughts.

The two friends sprinted out of the arcade on to the promenade. Billy glanced back over his shoulder. His heart raced at the sight of the five boys all haring after them.

Calum didn't speak. He panted heavily as his long legs opened up a short lead over Billy.

'YOU'RE DEAD MEAT!' a voice screamed from behind.

Billy sprinted on, his heart beating ever faster. Now he was at the side of his friend. He spoke in short gasps. 'They're going – to catch us – can't keep – this up –'

Calum still said nothing. His face was deathly white, his eyes wide with fear.

The sound of chasing footsteps grew louder. The two friends ran on, desperate to get away. They weaved in and out of the numerous holidaymakers strolling along the promenade. They almost knocked over a small boy walking between his parents.

'You stupid idiots!' the boy's father shouted after them.

They ran along a line of amusement arcades, side stalls, snack bars and on towards a small funfair at the end of the promenade.

Neither of them dared look back over their shoulder. They could hear the yobbish voices of their pursuers growing louder . . . They were sure to be caught – it was just a matter of time . . .

Billy stared ahead and saw a girl about the same age as himself walking straight towards him. She wore a black beret and a red tartan kilt. She was on a collision course.

'Get out of the way!' he yelled at her.

But she stared down at the ground and just kept on coming.

'WATCH OUT!'

He tried to swerve to miss her, but she moved the same way. He braced himself for the collision and half closed his eyes . . . but nothing happened! She wasn't there any more – and Billy found himself running onwards.

'The girl in the kilt!' Calum gasped. '*What happened?*'

Before Billy could reply, a hand gripped him on the shoulder. Without hesitation, he turned round and threw a punch with his right hand. It caught the youth completely by surprise and knocked him to the floor. The other four boys were close behind. The sight of their friend being punched to the ground made them madder than ever.

'YOU LITTLE . . .'

Billy didn't hear the rest. He and Calum ran on even faster than before . . . but they both knew they were almost finished.

And then . . . there in front, standing by the helter-skelter, a girl stood waving at them.

Billy and Calum gasped in surprise. It was the girl in the kilt again.

But how . . .

And then Billy recognized the girl's face . . .

Quick! This way!' she yelled at them.

She set off running to her right, and Billy and Calum followed. She led them through a maze of narrow streets and alleyways, all the time the voices of their pursuers growing more distant. Finally she led them up a narrow cobbled street that finished in a dead end.

They sat exhausted on the pavement by the side of an upturned shopping trolley.

Billy scanned around at the scattered beer cans and the graffiti on the wall. It was the same alleyway he'd seen earlier, right at the start of their walk. They'd run round in a huge loop. But it didn't matter. They'd shaken off their pursuers, lost them . . . and all due to their mysterious helper.

'This – is the girl – I told you about,' Billy said to Calum in short gasps.

'Your "dream girl",' Calum said sarcastically.

The girl didn't look up. She picked up an old lollipop stick and began breaking it into little pieces.

'Who are you?' Billy asked her.

'Bunty,' she replied. 'Bunty Watkins.'

'What sort of name's that?' Calum asked.

'What's your name?' the girl asked back.

'Calum!'

'Well what sort of name's that?' she sniggered.

Calum frowned.

'When you saw me at the station . . . you seemed to know me,' Billy said to her.

'I know lots of people . . . and lots of things,' Bunty said mysteriously.

'Look . . . we can't stay here,' Calum chipped in. 'Those guys will be looking for us.'

'You should go home, Calum . . . and you too, Billy. Go back to Aunt Emily's,' Bunty said calmly. 'They'll have forgotten about you by this afternoon.'

Calum jumped to his feet. 'Hey! How come you know his name?'

Bunty didn't reply. She threw the bits of lollipop stick into the gutter and started playing with the ends of her long blonde hair; it was greasy and matted.

Billy got to his feet, stood by Calum's side and stared down at her.

Her white roll-neck jumper looked grubby. Her kilt looked threadbare and both her white knee-length socks were full of holes. Her shoes were almost worn out and one of the silver buckles was hanging off.

Calum was also staring down at her. 'Your clothes are a bit retro, aren't they?' he said in a way that suggested they were a bit strange.

She still didn't look up. 'I don't know what you mean.'

Billy felt sorry for her. 'Where do you live?'

She glanced up and smiled. 'Not far from your auntie's.'

'How come you know so much?' Calum asked, his voice full of frustration.

Bunty rose to her feet and looked Calum squarely in the eyes. 'I told you before . . . I know lots of things –

because I'm a mermaid and I live on the bottom of the sea!' She ran down the alleyway, back towards the main road.

Calum looked at Billy with a pained expression. 'She's weird!'

'She saved us from that gang,' Billy pointed out. 'Come on . . . let's go after her.'

If Bunty wasn't the coolest dresser in town, she could certainly run. She sprinted all the way back to Auntie Emily's house and hardly drew breath as she stood by the gate.

'Come on, you two slowcoaches,' she teased them. 'What kept you?'

Bunty grinned. Her face looked radiant and her eyes blazed with energy.

Billy couldn't help admiring her. 'Do you want to hang around with us?' he asked.

'But she's . . . a girl!' Calum protested.

'Very observant, Calum Truelove!' Bunty laughed.

'Hey! How do you know . . .' Calum turned to Billy. 'I give up! This girl's a total nightmare!'

Billy nodded, and Bunty burst out laughing. She folded her arms across her chest. 'I suppose you think I'm just a girl and not very tough?' She bit into her bottom lip and looked thoughtful. 'Well, maybe you're right. But I *do* need your help, especially Billy's. That's why I'm here.'

'What do you mean?' Billy asked, beginning to tense. 'Why do you need our help?'

Bunty looked at him. 'I'll tell you tonight. Meet me by the old Punch and Judy stand – it's by the side of the pier – if you're brave enough!'

Billy didn't hesitate. 'What time?'

Bunty didn't hesitate either. 'Midnight!'

Billy and Calum looked at each other in disbelief.

Bunty began to walk away. 'That's settled then!'

'But why midnight?' Calum shouted after her.

'Because that's the only time I can show you,' she shouted back.

'Show us what?' Billy asked expectantly.

Bunty broke into a run. 'YOUR WORST NIGHTMARE!' she yelled over her shoulder.

And then she was gone.

4 Midnight Encounter

Later that afternoon, the two boys had moved their belongings upstairs into the spare bedroom. They were right next door to old Henry's bedroom. His door was closed, but every now and then they could hear him moving around.

And now Billy and Calum lay awake in the big double bed.

It had been easy to stay awake. There had been so much to talk about. As usual, Calum did most of the talking . . . his brain working overtime. 'What do you make of old Henry?' Calum whispered.

'He's a bit scary . . . but I think he's OK!' Billy replied.

'He's a *lot* scary!' Calum went on. 'He really gives me the creeps!'

'Keep your voice down,' Billy said quietly. 'He might be listening. He's only in the next room.'

'Probably with his ear to the wall,' Calum whispered in a creepy voice.

'I don't think so,' Billy chuckled. 'Listen . . .'

They both lay in silence and strained their ears. A rasping snore sounded through the wall. The boys giggled and resumed their conversation.

'What do you make of Bunty Watkins?' Calum said thoughtfully.

'I've never met anyone called Bunty before,' Billy whispered.

'Except you did meet her *before*,' Calum reminded him, 'twice, if your dreams are anything to go by. She makes me feel nervous. She's wacko!'

Billy giggled. 'It's like she's from a different planet, but I still like her.'

'Did you see what she was wearing?' Calum said laughing. 'She looked like some sort of miniature female Scotsman.'

Billy shrieked with laughter. Calum laughed even louder. They were almost laughing to the point of tears when a voice sounded from the doorway: 'Are you two settling down? It's time you were asleep.'

'Sorry, Aunt Emily,' Billy said, trying not to giggle.

'Well, goodnight then!'

'Goodnight!'

'Goodnight!' Calum repeated.

As Aunt Emily's footsteps retreated on to the landing, Calum leant out and looked at the electronic clock on the bedside cabinet. 11:45 pm.

'OK, Billy . . . it's almost time. We'll wait five more minutes, check your aunt's settled down, then we'll go.'

A knot suddenly formed in Billy's stomach. He decided he would much rather stay tucked up in bed than venture out into the cold night air and meet Bunty.

Billy and Calum walked with hands deep in pockets towards the seafront promenade.

The streets were dark and almost deserted. Just a few late-night revellers returning home, the occasional car driving past, everything quite normal.

'I hope those guys from the arcade aren't lurking around,' Calum said. 'It'd just be our luck to bump into them.'

'Just keep your head down and keep walking,' Billy replied. 'We're nearly there.'

'So you know where it is?'

'I can't remember seeing an old Punch and Judy stand, but I know where the pier is.'

'And do you think Bunty what's-her-name is really going to be there?' Calum asked.

'She'll be there,' Billy said confidently.

A thin, grey drizzle began to fall and the two boys sped up a little.

A few minutes later they were walking along the empty promenade. The sea was far out on their left and looked inky-black; the waves made a loud crashing sound as they broke on the shore.

'There's the pier,' Billy said, pointing ahead.

As they drew closer, a girl stepped out from the shadows of a tall wooden structure.

'You made it,' Bunty said. 'I wasn't sure you'd turn up.'

Calum looked at his watch. 'It's bang on midnight,' he whispered.

Loud voices sounded from across the road. A drunken gang stumbled out of a doorway and staggered away up the pavement.

'It's a disco – the Icelandic . . .' Bunty informed them.

Billy looked left towards the pier entrance. A sign by the side of a rusting turnstile read: 'PIER UNSAFE – CLOSED FOR REPAIRS'.

'We can't go in there,' Calum said. 'It's too dangerous.'

Bunty set off towards it, 'It's OK . . . I know what I'm doing. Billy – follow me!'

'What about me?' Calum asked indignantly. 'You're not leaving me behind.'

Billy stared at Bunty's shiny black coat. It looked like plastic. She pulled the collar up around her ears. He'd never seen a coat like that before. She was wearing the same beret she'd been wearing earlier. What with the black plastic coat and the beret, he thought she looked like some sort of secret agent.

'I'm going to show Billy his worst nightmare – the reason I need your help,' she said. 'I want you to stay here. Keep watch. We'll not be long. When Billy gets back, get him home.'

Billy turned to his friend. Calum didn't look at all pleased. 'I don't know what this is all about,' Billy frowned. 'Do you mind keeping a look out. If anyone comes –'

'I'll give a loud whistle with my fingers,' Calum interrupted. 'I suppose you're right . . . one of us needs to keep watch. If the police come and find you on that pier you'll be in serious trouble.'

Bunty smiled at Calum and moved towards the turnstile. She climbed over it and disappeared into the shadows. 'Come on, Billy!' she whispered from the darkness. 'Follow me!'

'OK . . . I'm coming!' He whispered over his shoulder, 'If we're not back in ten minutes, and you can't see any sign of us . . .'

'Don't worry,' Calum said in a reassuring tone of voice, 'I'll raise the alarm.'

Billy nodded and disappeared over the turnstile into the darkness.

If it was spooky in the streets, it was twice as spooky on the deserted run-down pier. Bunty led Billy through a maze of shadowy huts, the sea crashing loudly beneath their feet.

'Where are you taking me?'

'You'll see. Be patient!'

'If this is some sort of joke, then it's definitely not funny!'

'It's no joke!'

They walked up to an old wooden bench alongside the rusted pier railings. Bunty sat down on it and beckoned Billy to do the same. They sat side by side and she shuffled up to him.

'Hold my hands,' Bunty said, making Billy feel uncomfortable.

He began to stammer with embarrassment. 'B-but . . . why?'

'Hold both my hands and close your eyes . . . you'll see why!'

She closed her eyes. Billy hesitated. She opened her eyes, scowled at him, and then closed them again.

Billy got the message. 'OK . . . if you say so!' He took hold of her hands and gasped. They felt so cold . . . so hard . . . like ice! He closed his eyes.

'Now count to three!'

Billy took a deep breath and did as he was told. 'One . . . two . . . three!'

An intensity of light, life and sound suddenly exploded around him. Billy opened his eyes and gawped.

It was daylight – a warm, sunny day . . . lots of people walking among the brightly coloured stalls – Madame Zafira, – Fortune-Teller . . . Hot Dogs . . . Ices . . . Candyfloss – busy amusement arcades. A siren sounded from the end of the pier – a ghost train perhaps?

Billy looked at Bunty. She was smiling at him. He realized he was still holding her hands, but now they felt warm and soft. He let go and jumped back.

'This is a dream, isn't it? It's not really happening. It can't be!'

'I've got to go now, Billy. My mum's waiting. She's calling me. I'll catch up with you later.'

As Bunty got up, he noticed she was wearing the kilt again – the black plastic coat had disappeared. 'You can't just leave me here,' Billy pleaded. 'I need to get back to Calum.'

'Bunty gave Billy a warm smile. 'He'll be waiting for you after you've seen it.'

'Seen what?'

Bunty hesitated and her smile changed to a frown. 'How it all started . . . the reason why you're here to help me! It's waiting at the end of the pier.'

As Bunty disappeared into the crowd, Billy looked

around again. It was a happy peaceful scene with lots of people enjoying themselves. And yet there was something really strange about it all . . . something he couldn't quite put his finger on.

A child by his side dropped her ice cream cone on the floor and started crying. Her mum bent down and picked it up. Her skirt was so short that Billy looked away – he'd never seen a mum with a skirt so short – and it was made out of the same shiny plastic as Bunty's coat. And then Billy noticed that lots of people were wearing clothes he hadn't seen before.

His mind swirling in confusion, he got up and moved towards the end of the pier. If his worst nightmare was waiting for him, then it was time to go and face it.

He got up and made his way through the crowds of holidaymakers. The siren shrieked out again in the distance . . . excited screams – definitely a ghost train.

My worst nightmare . . . Surely she didn't mean the ghost train? Calum's right – she's crazy!

Billy relaxed a little and moved on more quickly.

And then he heard a different sound.

Laughter! High-pitched hysterical laughter! *Sinister, menacing . . . terrifying laughter!*

The sound of it filled Billy with dread. Goosebumps spread all over his body and a cold tingling sensation shot down his spine. He felt compelled to turn around and flee back to the pier entrance.

No! I'm Billy Hardacre. I'm not scared!

And with this brave thought surging through his mind, he pushed on towards the end of the pier.

5
Nightmare Experience

The horrible laughter was coming from inside a small arcade next to the ghost train. As Billy walked towards it, he saw the brightly-coloured sign above the entrance.

Scullion's Amusements

As Billy made his way slowly inside, the laughter stopped.

The arcade was full of slot machines – old-fashioned mechanical ones; not a single electronic machine in sight!

Billy watched as a boy put a coin into a slot, flicked a lever, and a small metal ball shot around a spiral coil before disappearing into a hole at the centre. The boy muttered and walked away. Another boy put a coin in a crane machine and tried to pick up a fluffy toy, but the jaws of the crane closed over thin air and missed the toy completely.

Billy pressed on, wondering what he was going to find, all the time growing more and more tense . . . *Then the hideous laughter started again.*

He swung around and saw the small figure over to his right. It was seated in a glass case, rocking from side to side. A boy about the same age as Billy stood and watched. A younger girl stood by his side – his sister, perhaps. She started to cry and stepped backwards.

Billy moved closer and saw that the figure was some sort of sailor doll sitting astride a barrel. It laughed hysterically, its hands planted on its knees and its eyes seeming to stare back at anyone who looked at it.

It suddenly stopped moving and its head dropped forward. The boy moved away and tried to console the young girl.

Billy walked up to the glass and peered at the slumped figure. It wore a navy-blue sailor suit, its cap resting carelessly on its head of wiry black hair.

Whoaahh . . . that is so spooky, Billy thought to himself.

He stared further and took in the doll's grotesque features – wide nose . . . flared nostrils . . . cheeks jutting out savagely . . . thick lips – all set in a hideous grin.

A man edged up to Billy's shoulder and laughed. 'You

do right to stare, son. That doll's enough to give anybody nightmares!'

Before Billy had chance to say anything, the man put a coin in the slot and stood back with his arms folded.

Billy was only inches away from the glass as the doll's head angled upwards. Its eyes were only painted – but they seemed to stare at him with frightening ferocity. As the doll sprang to life, he jumped backwards.

'Steady on, son . . . it's only a doll!'

But as the demonic laughter grew louder and the intense eyes followed his every move, Billy sensed that this was much more than a harmless doll. Bunty knew it too . . . she hadn't sent him here for nothing.

He began to panic. His mind swirled in a confusion of thoughts and images – slot machines, hot dog stands, candyfloss stalls, and brightly-coloured lights. He began to feel dizzy. He started to fall backwards . . . in slow motion . . . a fainting movement. He hit the floorboards with a heavy thump and everything went black.

And when he opened his eyes . . . *everyone had disappeared*!

He sat up by the side of the slot machine. All was silent. The sailor doll had lapsed back into lifelessness. Billy held his breath, sensing that something awful was about to happen. Still feeling faint, he struggled to his feet. He had to get back to Calum.

As he walked away, the hideous laughter started up

again. He looked anxiously over his shoulder . . . *and his blood froze.*

The sailor doll was rising to its feet.

Like a rabbit frozen in a car headlight, Billy stood rooted to the spot . . . watching everything happen . . . unable to do anything.

With its eyes firmly fixed on Billy, the doll threw a punch and shattered its glass prison into a thousand fragments. It began climbing out of the slot machine and down towards the floor. At first its movements were jerky, mechanical . . . unreal. But as it reached the floor and turned its head, it moved in a more human way, like a small child.

Billy finally reacted. He turned and started to run.

He ran and ran, weaving his way through the shadows . . . the pier dark and deserted again. He almost tripped over a cat that sprang out from behind a hut, and then he bumped into a waste bin. But there was no time to pause. The nightmarish laughter was growing louder all the time.

Billy finally reached the pier entrance, saw the turnstile and lunged at it, throwing himself over the top and out on to the promenade . . . and then all was darkness – grey, damp, drizzly darkness – as he fainted again.

When he came round, Calum was kneeling over him.

'Are you OK, Billy? Are you all right?'

'Why? What happened?'

'You passed out. You must have climbed over the turnstile, fell on to the pavement and banged your head. I found you in a crumpled heap.'

Billy felt his head. No bumps. No soreness. 'I think I'm OK. What happened?'

Calum looked at him with a guilty expression. 'I'm not sure. I fell asleep . . . I only woke up when you came crashing through the turnstile –' Calum paused '– and that's when I realized . . .'

'Realized what?' Billy asked, a nervous flutter welling up in his stomach.

'It's four o'clock in the morning! You were in there for four hours!'

Billy felt the colour drain from his cheeks. 'Wow!' was all he could say at first. His mind reeled back to the events inside. 'Did anyone – anything – follow me out?'

'I don't think so . . . I didn't see anyone. What happened in there? Where's Bunty?'

Billy struggled to his feet. 'I'm freezing. Let's get back to Aunt Emily's. I'll tell you everything then. You'll never believe it!'

Calum scanned nervously around. 'I'll believe anything you tell me, Billy-boy!'

Billy walked up to the turnstile and peered through on to the pier. Everything was clothed in shadows, dark and deserted . . . no sign of anything untoward. He shook his head in disbelief.

'Come on! Let's go!' he sighed. 'The sooner we're back, the better!'

The streets were empty. Not even a car to be seen. They were completely alone . . . but Billy kept glancing over his shoulder, as if someone might be following.

'Billy . . . why do you keep looking behind?'

'You don't want to know,' Billy said. 'Just keep walking. We need to get back.'

Calum nodded nervously and lengthened his stride . . . Billy found himself jogging to keep up.

Suddenly every sound and every shadow seemed threatening.

Overturned dustbins cast shadows of creeping monsters on graffiti-covered walls and a cat screamed the scream of a preying vampire. Billy and Calum walked on nervously, neither of them speaking.

They turned away from the promenade into a dark street and saw a long row of wheely bins lined up along the kerbside. As they sped past, Calum tapped each one with his left hand. Billy guessed it was just a nervous reaction.

Neither of the boys saw the lid of the fourth bin rise up a little as Calum's hand knocked against it.

6
Street Stalker

Further along the road, Billy stopped in his tracks and looked over his shoulder.

'What's up?' Calum asked.

Billy stared down the deserted street, along the line of wheely bins. 'There's something wrong! I can sense it!'

'Billy, you're freaking me out,' Calum uttered. He sped on, Billy racing after him. A loud clatter sounded some distance behind.

Billy stopped and swung round. Calum did the same. A wheely bin at the bottom of the road had toppled over. Something was moving by the side of it.

Calum's voice started to quake, 'It's just a cat . . .'

'It's no cat!' Billy whispered. 'Quick! Get down!' He tugged at Calum's elbow. They dived into a gateway and peered around the hedge down the street.

They watched in stunned silence as a small child-sized figure delved into the rubbish spilt from the wheely bin and began throwing it over the privet hedge into the garden.

'God! Who's that?' Calum asked in disbelief.

'You don't want to know!' Billy muttered half under his breath.

When the sinister silhouetted figure had scattered all of the bin's contents into the garden, it picked up something heavy from the gutter and threw it towards the house. Billy looked at Calum in horror as the sound of breaking glass reached their ears.

The dwarf-like figure sprinted away down the street. At the same time, the lights came on in several of the windows.

'We'd better get out of here fast or they'll think it's us!' Billy exclaimed. 'Run for it!'

Calum was in no mood to argue and they set off at full speed. This was becoming a habit! They sprinted around the corner into the next street. Almost back!

Billy glanced nervously up the alleyway where they'd sat with Bunty that morning. He saw a small figure scurry across a dark space and retreat into the shadows. A shiver rattled down his spine. 'Did you see that?' he gasped. 'Something's creeping around up there!'

Calum shuddered. 'Let's get back . . . I've had enough excitement for one night!'

Billy nodded and sprinted on. He'd definitely had more than enough.

They finally reached Aunt Emily's and breathed a sigh of relief. No lights on . . . everything in darkness. They hadn't been missed.

Billy was the first through the front door. Calum followed, looking distinctly pale. They crept upstairs and into the bedroom. Neither spoke as they slipped out of their clothes and back into their pyjamas.

'I feel tired out and scared stiff at the same time,' Calum whispered. 'Now tell me – what happened on that pier?'

'OK,' Billy replied, climbing into bed and snuggling down under the duvet. 'And then we'd better try and get some sleep – we're going to need it!'

Calum nodded and climbed in beside him. Billy closed his eyes and relived the whole experience. He told Calum everything.

Calum lay in stunned silence and said nothing until Billy had finished. 'Wow! No wonder you couldn't wait to get back here. That sailor doll sounds more scary than the Bonebreaker!'

'When you found me and I came round, I thought it had all been a dream – some sort of vision – but I'm not so sure now.'

'Well Bunty was real enough,' Calum said. 'I wonder what happened to her.'

Billy yawned. 'I don't know. Let's talk about it tomorrow. Like I said . . . we need to get some sleep.'

Calum nodded and turned over. Billy closed his eyes and tried desperately to empty his mind of all that had happened. He finally managed to drop off.

When he opened his eyes again, it was still dark and Calum was snoring beside him. He wasn't sure why he'd woken up – he didn't need the loo or anything. He just sensed that something was wrong. He peered over his duvet around the bedroom. All was cloaked in shadows, but otherwise everything was as it should be.

He slipped out of bed and crept out on to the landing. He peered down the stairs and his heart leapt at the sight of the front door half open.

Calum must have forgot to drop the latch, he thought to himself. He trod quietly down the stairway, gently closed the door and dropped the latch.

A few minutes later he was back in bed . . . still feeling that something was very wrong.

Oh no! he suddenly thought to himself. *If the door's been open, something might have got in!*

He looked around the bedroom again . . . everything still quite normal. He broke out in goosebumps as he made his mind up to look under the bed. He leant out, lowered his head and peered into the dark space.

Every muscle in his body went completely stiff as he

saw the small figure lying there, its head turning towards him in the half-light.

Billy leapt back up and almost knocked Calum out of bed. 'CALUM! HELP!'

Calum groaned, still half asleep. 'What are you on about?'

'You left the door open . . . *It's got in . . . under the bed!'*

As Calum's brain registered what Billy was trying to say, his face went a deathly shade of white. He took a deep breath and leant over his own side of the bed. He straightened up again and faced Billy. 'What are you on about? There's nothing there!'

Billy leant over again on his own side. Sure enough, whatever he'd seen a few minutes earlier had gone!

'You've had a nightmare, Billy! Try and get back to sleep.'

Billy laid his head back on the pillow, his heart still racing. Calum was right – these days it was hard to tell the difference between dreams and reality!

He took one last look over the edge of his duvet . . . *and saw the silhouette of the small figure standing at the bottom of his bed!*

It jumped on to the duvet and began crawling up his legs. Billy watched in shocked horror as the grinning wooden face with red cheeks inched its way up towards his chest. He tried to scream, but the sailor doll had already reached out and gripped him by the neck. '*Calum . . .*' Billy croaked. He dug his elbow heavily into Calum's ribs.

Calum stirred. 'What's up now?'

Billy couldn't answer . . . he was choking.

Calum jolted upright and sprang into action. He lashed out at the sailor doll, but it never budged. It sat astride Billy's chest, its thick bushy eyebrows and wiry black hair giving it a grotesque appearance . . . wooden chubby fingers closing ever tighter around his throat.

Billy felt faint as the lack of oxygen took effect.

Calum jumped out of bed, lifted his side of the duvet and threw it over the demonic figure. Thrust into darkness, the doll released its grip – and Calum wrapped it tight and pushed it over Billy's side of the bed on to the floor.

Coughing and spluttering, Billy jumped out on to his 'mummified' enemy and sat on it, pinning it to the ground. The doll struggled and writhed, wrapped up inside the heavy duvet.

'Through the window!' Calum yelled.

Billy nodded. As Calum opened the window, he lifted the rolled-up duvet and manhandled it through. He watched as the bundle fell down into the garden and landed heavily.

'WHAT ON EARTH ARE YOU DOING?' a voice boomed from behind.

He turned round to see Aunt Emily glaring at him. 'I'm . . . I'm . . . sorry!' Billy stammered. 'Something got in . . . under the bed. Me and Calum–'

'Calum looks frozen!' Aunt Emily interrupted. 'Whatever possessed you to pull the duvet off and throw it through the window?'

Billy looked at the bed. Calum was sitting up and staring at him in a very peculiar way. 'He's been dreaming again!' Calum said indignantly.

'But . . . but . . . you saw . . .'

Calum yawned and stretched his arms. 'The only thing I saw was you, wrestling with the duvet. Why did you chuck it out of the window?'

Billy leant out of the window and looked down into the garden. The duvet lay where it landed, still rolled up. He turned back to Calum, and then to Aunt Emily. It seemed that Calum was right – he'd been dreaming again! 'Sorry!' was all Billy could think to say. 'I've had a nightmare.'

As Aunt Emily tutted and accused Billy of watching too many scary videos, he put his slippers on and headed downstairs to retrieve the duvet. On the way, he tried to sort out in his mind the dreams from the reality. The business on the pier had seemed real enough at the time. But so had the sailor doll under the bed. And what about the dwarf-like figures in the street on the way home? Calum had seen them, surely?

Well, nightmares or not, Billy was sure of one thing – *it was all a warning of things to come.*

7
Initial Enquiries

Billy and Calum dressed and went downstairs to the smell of bacon and eggs.

'Smells fantastic!' Calum said.

'Come on, you two!' Aunt Emily greeted them. 'Sit yourselves down. Breakfast's about ready. I'll get you fed and then I'll have to be off to work soon.'

A few minutes later, the two friends were seated at the table, tucking into one of Aunt Emily's fry-ups. Henry was there, sipping milk off the end of his spoon, every now and then taking a slurp from a large mug of tea.

'Are you OK now, Billy?' Aunt Emily asked him. 'I never heard a peep from your room until you decided to throw the duvet out of the window. You both seemed to have slept well until then.'

Billy cast a glance at Calum. Calum returned the same guilty look. Henry stopped sipping from his spoon and stared in Billy's direction, his eyes big and challenging. 'Have you ever seen a slot machine with a spooky kind of sailor doll inside?' Billy asked all at once.

Henry suddenly coughed . . . choked on his breakfast. He took a handkerchief from his pocket and wiped his mouth.

'Are you OK, Henry?' Aunt Emily asked, her voice full of concern.

Henry nodded, but said nothing.

'The laughing sailor!' Aunt Emily continued. She placed a plate of toast on the table and looked into space. 'I remember them well. Most of the arcades had them.' She shuddered and smiled at the same time. 'They used to give me nightmares – and my friends – hideous things. It was the eyes . . . they seemed to follow you around. And that laugh . . . it sent a shiver down your spine. Thank God they've all gone now. I can't imagine why anyone would think they were amusing.'

All went silent around the table.

Calum looked at Billy curiously and took up the questioning. 'We bumped into some lads yesterday, wearing red baseball caps. They seemed like real trouble. I wondered if they were the vandals you told us about.'

Henry coughed again and cleared his throat. 'I've seen 'em. Damn yobs. It wouldn't have 'appened in my day.

They'd 'ave been straight in the army . . . that would 'ave sorted 'em out!'

Aunt Emily smiled. She looked from Henry to Calum and stroked her chin. 'Yes. I've seen them. They're a bad lot. You're probably right, but nobody can ever catch them at it.'

Billy looked sheepishly towards Calum.

'And there's a girl we've met. She wears a kilt and a beret,' Calum continued. 'She's called Bunty . . . Bunty Watkins.'

Henry's face turned ashen. He got up and left.

'I wonder what rattled him,' Aunt Emily said, shaking her head. She stroked her chin again. 'Bunty, you said her name was. That's real old-fashioned name. It doesn't ring any bells.'

She poured the boys a cup of tea and looked curiously at them. 'Anything else you want to know? Seems to me you've been reading too many mystery books.

Billy smiled. He didn't read much but he liked mysteries.

'So what are your plans for today?' Aunt Emily asked, beginning to clear away the plates.

Billy got up to help. 'I'm not sure. What do you want to do, Cal?'

'Why don't you go down to the lifeboat station on the North Landing?' Aunt Emily suggested. 'It's an interesting place. You can have a look around and they won't charge you a penny. You'll see all the old photos of your Uncle Jack.'

'And we can explore the caves in the cove,' Billy added. 'What do think, Cal?'

Calum rubbed his hands together. 'I'm up for it . . . it sounds a great idea.'

Billy was the first to step outside. The weather was still cold and grey, but a few patches of blue sky showed in the distance. Perhaps it would cheer up later.

He put his hands into his pockets and pulled out the little hat. He'd forgotten all about it.

'What's that?' Calum asked.

'It's that weird little sailor hat that we found among the rubbish. I know this sounds mad . . . but what if it's one of those dolls that's causing the problems – the vandalism.'

Calum looked back at him with wide eyes. 'You can't be serious?'

'I know it sounds crazy . . . but it's no more crazy than the Bonebreaker business.'

Both boys allowed their minds to wander back to the seven-foot tall Viking phantom. Calum nodded in agreement. 'That's true . . . this holiday is getting spookier by the minute, just like last time. Come on – we'll go through everything again on the way, and we'll check out that alleyway and the house where the window got smashed.'

They walked on and soon reached the narrow passage where Billy had spotted the sinister small figure scurrying amongst the shadows.

'There was definitely something moving around up there last night,' Billy said.

Calum walked up the alleyway and headed towards an upturned supermarket trolley. 'Wow! Take a look at this!'

Billy joined him. They stood side by side and gawped at the familiar image daubed on the wall – a wheely bin with a pair of sinister eyes peering out from the dark space below the lid, the word 'SCULLION' written diagonally down the side of the bin.

'It's same as the ones we saw at the side of the railway track,' Calum uttered in surprise. 'What does it mean?'

'I've seen that word somewhere else,' Billy remarked.

'Where?'

'Can't remember!'

'Come on! Try! It might be important.'

Billy concentrated hard . . . and then it came to him. 'The end of the pier . . . the arcade with the sailor doll . . . it had Scullion's name painted over it.'

'Interesting,' Calum said. 'Let's go and take a look at that house further down the street.'

They passed by the terraced house where the spooky little figure had jumped out of the wheely bin. They looked across and saw the boarded-up window. The front door opened and an old woman appeared on the doorstep.

'What are you two gawping at?'

'Nothing!' Calum shouted back.

The old woman glared back at them. 'Someone broke my window – early this morning. Yobs and vandals – the town's full of 'em! It fair gave me a heart attack.' The woman started down the path towards them, her arms folded across her chest. 'Don't suppose you two know anything about it?'

'No idea!' Calum said, quickly walking on. 'We're here on holiday.'

'Just for half term,' Billy added.

'Well see you keep yourselves out of trouble!' the woman snapped at them. 'We've got quite enough of it as it is!' She headed back into the house and slammed the door.

'What do you reckon?' Billy asked.

'Well . . . whoever did it looked small . . . like . . .'

'. . . one of those sailor dolls I saw on the pier, and in my nightmare!' Billy finished for him.

'So you really believe that those things are causing the trouble?'

Billy's mind went back to the horrific events of the night before. 'I don't know. Last night all seemed like a horrible dream . . . like it wasn't real?'

'Well, whatever broke that window was real enough,' Calum stated sternly.

'Let's get on to the lifeboat station.'

Billy nodded. This half-term holiday was growing crazier by the minute and it was anybody's guess what might happen next.

8

Heroes of the Sea

As they approached one of the many snack bars, Billy reached into his pocket and took out the money Aunt Emily had given him. 'Fancy an ice cream?'

Calum nodded enthusiastically and decided on a Taste Blaster ice-lolly, while Billy settled for a double ripple choc-ice. They walked on contentedly, gazing around.

'Look!' Calum whispered to Billy. 'That's the arcade with the Zombie Attack . . . where that gang hang out.'

As they walked past, Billy peered in. He caught his breath as he saw the back of a red baseball cap opposite the screen.

Calum saw it too. 'Quick! Let's move on.'

They slunk past and trod quietly. The gang didn't see them.

Just beyond the funfair, the blue-and-orange flag of

the lifeboat station blew in the breeze. 'Do you think we might bump into Bunty?' Calum asked.

Billy shrugged his shoulders. 'You never know. She could turn up anywhere.'

'Why do you think she wears such funny clothes?'

'No idea . . . she's strange.'

Calum nodded. He slurped the last remnants of his Taste Blaster ice-lolly and threw the stick into a waste bin.

A minute later, the sun came out and suddenly everything seemed cheerier.

The two boys walked on without speaking, taking in the scene – smiling faces, mouthwatering smells of hot dogs and candyfloss, waves breaking gently on the beach below . . . so much better than being at school. Bliss!

As they approached the funfair, Billy stared up at the huge Ferris wheel. It dwarfed the helter-skelter by its side. But it was the ghost train that attracted the attentions of the two friends the most.

'Wow! That looks seriously scary!' Calum said, stopping in his tracks.

'This is new,' Billy said. 'It's a lot bigger than the one that used to be on the pier.'

The two friends sauntered up and stared in awe at the spooky artwork adorning the walls of the ride – grinning skeletons, flying witches and a train driver that looked like a cross between a zombie and a vampire.

'Shall we give it a go?' Calum asked, rooting through his pockets. 'I've got a pound coin somewhere.'

'I've still got some change from the money Aunt Emily gave me. We'll have a go now and then move on to the lifeboat station.'

A loud siren screamed from somewhere inside the ghost train and Billy's heart skipped a beat. A nervous feeling suddenly welled up in his stomach.

Calum looked at him. 'Are you OK, Billy? Your face has gone as white as a sheet.'

'I . . . I feel a bit weird,' Billy croaked.

Calum stared, his eyes wide. 'What's wrong?'

Billy didn't reply. He had a sudden urge to look over his shoulder. He spotted the red baseball caps in the distance . . . moving towards them. He grabbed Calum's arm. 'Quick! Get on!'

Calum did as he was told and climbed into the front carriage of the ghost train. A man with greasy black hair and an even greasier bushy black beard took their money.

'Hold on tight you guys . . . it gets really scary in there.' He grinned at them.

As the train lurched forward and crashed through the doors, Billy glanced back and saw the gang walking past . . . they hadn't seen them.

Calum glanced back at the same time. 'So that's why you were panicking – the "Red Cap Gang"!'

Billy said nothing. He clung tight to the handrail and took a deep breath.

The churning feeling in his stomach was still there.

The train plunged into the darkness. Fluorescent phantoms barred their way . . . always disappearing at the last second. A spooky graveyard appeared at the side of the track. As the train glided by, a coffin opened and a vampire with bloodstained fangs sat up and stared at them.

'Hey . . . this is brilliant,' Calum yelled from Billy's side.

Billy didn't answer. He sensed that something awful was about to happen.

The train careered on into the darkness. A fake thunderstorm lit up a spooky castle painted on the wall in front of them.

But it was something else that suddenly attracted their attention.

Calum screamed out first, 'There's something on the track . . . running towards us!'

'IT'S A SAILOR DOLL!' Billy shrieked.

Billy gripped the handrail even tighter and braced himself. The dwarf-like figure charged at them, leapt over the front of the carriage and grabbed Billy by the neck. The lights went out and Billy screamed in pain as the doll sank its teeth into one of his ears.

'Get it off!' Billy shrieked.

As the train lurched around another corner, Calum struggled to pull the dwarfish attacker away from Billy's body. At the same time, Billy pushed for all he was worth, until the doll finally lost its grip and toppled back over the front of the engine. The sound of crunching splintering wood competed with a screaming siren. Clutching his ear, Billy looked back and saw the smashed sailor doll lying lifeless across the rails. A few seconds later, the train crashed back through the doors into welcome daylight, marking the end of the ride.

Billy's instincts had been right. Danger had been lurking . . . and it hadn't been the Red Cap Gang!

'That was nasty!' Billy gasped as they walked away.

Calum wiped the sweat off his forehead. 'Somebody's definitely got it in for us.'

'Billy! Your aunt's lodger . . . look!'

Billy looked eagerly ahead. Calum was right – it was Henry, sitting on a bench by the side of the lifeboat station. He was reading a newspaper and hadn't seen them. They crept past him and made their way through the entrance.

The lifeboat loomed over them, taking up most of the space in the huge wooden building. It looked impressive – powerful, streamlined and a clean as a new pin. Billy thought it looked brand new. The orange and blue colours were striking in contrast.

All around the lifeboat, the walls of the building were covered in framed pictures. Some showed newspaper cuttings of rescues. Others displayed photographs of lifeboat crews, tracing the station's history.

Billy walked along the lines of photographs, studying each one carefully. Calum didn't seem interested. He just wanted to talk about what had happened on the ghost train.

'That thing must have been following us,' Calum pointed out, scratching his chin. 'But how can a doll move like that? And why did it attack us? What's going on?'

Billy didn't answer. He was too absorbed with a photograph of a small boat in distress. The scene was dramatic; the boat was being tossed about in a huge sea under a heavy grey sky. He could almost sense the fear of the crew. And on the edge of the photograph, an even smaller boat . . . *the lifeboat*!

Calum stopped muttering and looked up at the photograph. 'I'm glad I wasn't out there on that night,' he said solemnly.

Another photograph at the side showed a man with his arms folded in a pose. Billy recognized the man's striking features immediately. A gold earring hung from one of his ears; Billy decided it gave his uncle a film-star image.

'Is that your Uncle Jack?' Calum asked, straining to read the caption beneath the photo.

Before Billy had chance to reply, he felt a heavy hand on his shoulder and his heart turned to ice.

'Quite the hero, your uncle!' the old man said quietly.

Billy turned, saw Henry and sighed with relief. The sight of Aunt Emily's lodger was far more welcome than one of the dreaded sailor dolls or a member of the Red Cap Gang.

'Sorry if I startled you, lad,' Henry said apologetically. 'I was out having a stroll and I saw you and your pal walk in here. I thought I'd see what you were up to.'

The boys looked back to the picture. 'Was he out there . . . Billy's uncle?' Calum asked.

Henry stared at the photograph with sad, hollow eyes. 'He was . . . and he never came back. The Great Storm – he gave his life for those heathens!'

Billy looked from the photograph to Henry's bitter expression. 'Which heathens?'

The old man sounded more bitter than ever. 'The smugglers!'

Calum's eyes blazed with interest. 'What smugglers?'

'Scullion and his men,' Henry replied in an angry voice.

'That name again,' Billy said. 'The amusement arcade . . . at the end of the pier.'

'And the graffiti . . .' Calum added. 'Who is Scullion?' he asked, looking straight into Henry's face.

'You don't want to know – scum of the earth . . .'

Billy stared at Calum. Calum stared back.

Henry sauntered towards the exit. 'Don't be late for your tea. Emily's doing one of her steak and mushroom pies . . . six o'clock sharp, mind.'

'That name . . . "Scullion",' Calum said. 'It keeps cropping up.'

Billy dabbed his ear with his handkerchief – it was still throbbing and bleeding a little. 'I know! He sounds like bad news!'

They walked around the rest of the lifeboat station and found numerous photos of Billy's uncle. He really had been a hero and had been awarded two medals for bravery before losing his life on that fateful night.

'Hey, listen to this!' Calum said. He tugged at Billy's elbow and pulled him towards a newspaper cutting.

SCAWLSBY MAN ARRESTED AFTER SEA RESCUE

During a dramatic sea rescue by the Scawlsby Lifeboat Crew, several men lost their lives, including Jack Slater, a much-respected member of the crew for over seventeen years. It later transpired that the rescued boat was a smugglers' boat delivering drugs from the continent.

Mr Samuel Scullion, owner of the vessel, was subsequently arrested and charged along with other members of the crew. He is now in custody awaiting trial.

'So my uncle died trying to save drug smugglers!' Billy sighed.

Calum nodded. 'Looks like it! Come on . . . let's move on.'

But Billy wanted to spend more time looking over the impressive boat and all the photos and pictures on display.

'There's a first-aid post back up by the funfair. I think you should get that ear seen to,' Calum said in his sensible voice.

'And what do we say happened?' Billy replied sarcastically.

'A dog! It jumped up and bit you,' Calum suggested.

Billy dabbed his ear again. 'Would a dog really jump up and bite my ear?'

'Well . . . it could have been a big dog!' A different voice sounded from the entrance. 'It could've been a Great Dane!'

Billy's eyes lit up at the sight of the familiar beret crowning the smiling face. 'Bunty!' he cried out, perhaps a little too enthusiastically. He looked at Calum and blushed.

Calum frowned. 'She's in her mini-Scotsman outfit again!'

Bunty stood in the doorway; the pattern on her kilt looked striking in the sunlight. Billy chuckled to himself.

'Come on!' Bunty shouted to them. 'I want to take you somewhere.'

'Not to see his worst nightmare!' Calum replied sarcastically. 'We've just destroyed it.'

Bunty smiled knowingly. She didn't look at all surprised. 'No – I'm going to show you two more nightmares . . . Now get a move on!'

Calum scratched his head. 'This girl is seriously loopy!'

'But seriously interesting!' Billy added, a nervous flutter invading his stomach again. 'Let's get after her – before she disappears.'

9
Scullion's Cave

The two friends followed Bunty to the stone steps at the edge of the promenade. They leapt down the steps two at a time. When they reached the bottom, Bunty turned to face them. She looked straight at Billy, her big green eyes blazing with energy. 'So what did you think about that business on the end of the pier?'

Billy's mind swirled. There was so much he wanted to know. 'Did it really happen?' he asked. 'Or was it all a dream? The sailor doll that broke out of the slot machine –'

'And the ones we saw on the way home,' Calum interrupted. 'Billy dreamt that one of them got into the house under our bed –'

'And one's just attacked us on the ghost train,' Billy joined in again. 'And that was definitely no dream!' He pointed to his ear. At the same time, he fumbled in his pocket and took out the sailor cap. He held it up for Bunty to see. 'Look! We found this in the garden. Those dolls are running riot through the town, aren't they? I think it's time you told us –'

Before they could say any more, Bunty cut them off. 'I call them Dawn Demons. I took you to the pier to show you what they look like. It was a vision, Billy . . . formed from Scullion's evil power. It lurks there. I knew you would see it. It's something you're good at. That's why I picked you out.'

'Good at what?' Calum asked on Billy's behalf. 'And what do you mean "picked him out"?'

Billy stood there with his mouth open, waiting for Bunty's reply.

'Good at seeing things that other people can't. Visions . . . signs . . . tuning in to spirits and all that! That's why I picked on him – because I need someone like Billy to help me.'

'What's she on about?' Calum said.

'She's right!' Billy said thoughtfully. 'She means I'm like Mum. Mum has dreams – like me. She reads tealeaves and tells the future and all that stuff.'

Calum turned to face him and nodded. 'Do you think that's why the Bonebreaker picked on you?' he said.

'Well . . . I thought it was just because me and the Saxon boy were related, but there could be more to it,'

Billy replied. 'Maybe I *can* tune in to spirits.'

Bunty turned and started skipping across the firm wet sand. 'And maybe they can tune into you, Billy Hardacre – *especially the bad ones*! Come on! Follow me!' she said. And then she started singing:

> *'I'm a little mermaid*
> *Living in the sea*
> *Down on the bottom*
> *Where you can't find me.'*

Billy and Calum looked at each other in disbelief.

She ran some distance ahead and they watched as she took her off her beret and threw it into the wind. It glided across the beach like a frisbee. It hovered over their heads and they raced to catch it. Calum, being taller than Billy, managed to outstretch him and catch it cleanly in his left hand.

Bunty cried out from the distance, her long blonde hair blowing back in the offshore breeze. 'CLEVER BOY!' She ran across the vast expanse of firm sand, beyond where the promenade ended, and into a cove.

'Where's she taking us?' Calum asked, placing the beret on his head.

Billy roared with laughter. 'You look so stupid! She's taking us right where I was heading . . . to the caves, by the look of it.'

As Bunty continued to wave in the distance, a young woman walked towards them with a large dog. She smiled as she passed and the dog wagged its tail. Billy walked on and found himself looking down at the woman's footprints and the dog's pawprints, fresh in the moist sand. And then he looked behind at his own footprints curving back towards the promenade, and Calum's slightly bigger footprints, mingling with his own where they'd tried to catch Bunty's beret.

'HURRY UP, YOU TWO!' Bunty cried out from the distance. 'TIDE WILL BE IN SOON . . . AND THEN IT'LL BE TOO LATE!'

Billy looked towards her . . . looked down at the two sets of footprints again, the woman's and the dog's . . . *and then it struck him . . .*

'You've gone quiet again,' Calum said, still wearing the beret.

Billy stopped dead in his tracks and stared forward. 'She's not leaving any footprints!'

'Who isn't?'

'Bunty!'

Billy watched as Calum studied the sand. He looked back and glanced all around. The two boys gazed at each other. The approaching waves suddenly seemed very loud and threatening.

'Come on!' Billy said, snapping them back to reality. 'We need to ask that girl some more questions.'

Bunty had moved on towards three caves in the base of the chalk cliffs. Various groups of holidaymakers moved in and out of the enticing shadowy entrances, eager to explore and investigate.

As Billy and Calum drew nearer, the firm wet sand gave way to limestone ridges interlaced with rock pools. They moved on towards Bunty, passing small bands of explorers, and on towards a more distant cave in a narrow gully, which seemed to be ignored. A large notice board sticking out of the sand told them the reason why: 'BEWARE! RISING TIDES! DO NOT GO BEYOND THIS POINT!'

Bunty ignored it, walked on up the narrow inlet and stood at the entrance to the cave. Billy and Calum finally caught up.

'Why have you brought us here?' Calum complained. 'We can't go in there!'

The entrance to the cave was completely boarded up with a huge piece of plywood, the words 'DANGER! KEEP OUT!' painted across it in big white letters.

Bunty sat on a rock and looked up at them. 'They're in there . . .'

Calum passed her beret back. Billy stared at her. She wasn't smiling any more and this made him feel uneasy. 'Who are?'

'The Dawn Demons!'

Billy looked towards the boarded-up entrance and a

shiver rattled down his spine. His ear began to throb again . . . maybe he should have gone to the first-aid post after all.

'This is Scullion's Cave,' Bunty said, standing up and staring at the entrance.

'What do you know about Scullion?' Calum asked.

'He was a bad man,' she answered. 'Everyone in Scawlsby hated him. But nobody as much as me and Mum.'

Calum continued the questioning. 'Why did you hate him so much?'

Bunty picked up a stick and began to draw in a patch of wet sand trapped in between some limestone ridges. 'He took all our money . . . all our furniture . . . everything!'

Calum knelt beside her. His tone became more sympathetic. 'Why?'

'Mum had loaned some money from him and he wanted it back . . . but she couldn't pay . . . so he took everything. At first, he took our furniture, but even that wasn't enough. So then he turned us out of our house. Mum was desperate. She had no one to turn to. She didn't know what to do. We had nowhere to go.'

Billy looked at Bunty's face. For the first time she looked really sad as tears began to well up in her eyes.

'This is *his* cave,' she said, her voice suddenly filling with bitterness. 'He hid his stuff in here.'

'What stuff?' Calum asked.

'Cigarettes . . . beer and wine . . . that sort of stuff at first. And then they started smuggling drugs. His men landed their boats here at night and they hid it in the cave until it was safe to get rid of it.'

'Wow! Real smugglers!' Calum exclaimed.

Billy was still staring at the boarded-up cave entrance, fearing what might be lurking on the other side.

'So how much do you know about the sailor dolls?' he asked.

'They're controlled by him, by Scullion,' Bunty replied, still drawing in the sand. 'He brings them to life and makes them do evil things.'

'How can anyone control dolls?' Calum stammered.

'Especially when they're dead!' Billy added.

'Dead in body, but alive in spirit,' Bunty said grimly.

'And how many of these "Dawn Demons" are there?' Billy asked, hardly daring to hear the answer.

Calum looked down to where Bunty had been scribbling in the sand. 'Nine,' he replied for her.

Billy stopped forward and saw the nine stick men she'd drawn in the sand.

'There were ten, but you've already got rid of one on the ghost train.'

Billy gestured towards the cave. 'I suppose there are more of them are hiding in there?'

'Yes, two. The Dawn Demons are holed up all around

the town. I know their hiding places. They lie low during the day and he sends them out at dawn – the quietest time – to wreck the town.'

'But why . . .'

The waves crashed ever more loudly behind them.

'No more time,' Bunty interrupted. 'The tide's coming in fast. We need to get in there and sort them creeps out. Are you up for it?'

'I am if you are,' Billy said.

Calum didn't look so sure. He looked across at Bunty. 'Just how dangerous are they?'

'Very dangerous! That's why I waited for you both – especially you, Billy. We need to work together – like a team.'

She stood up, scanned around and walked over to a clump of rocks. She picked up a piece of driftwood with two rusty nails stuck out of one end. 'Come on then . . . there's not much time. Get yourselves a weapon. Let's see if we can reduce Scullion's army to seven!'

'But how can we get in?' Calum asked. 'It's all boarded up.'

Bunty walked up to the plywood board and reached down to the corner. 'The same way *they* get in . . . and out.'

Billy and Calum watched as she pulled on the board, making a gap between the wood and the limestone; it was just big enough for a child – *or a sailor doll* – to crawl through.

'Blimey . . . I don't fancy going in there,' Calum gasped, peering through into the darkness. 'How will we see?'

Bunty reached into the leather bag hanging from the belt of her kilt. 'With these . . .'

She took out two pencil torches and passed them to Billy and Calum.

'What about you?' Billy asked.

'I don't need one.'

As the tide roared even louder behind them, Billy and Calum followed Bunty's example and armed themselves with a stout piece of driftwood, each with nails sticking out from their ends.

Taking a deep breath, Billy crawled through the small gap and led the way into the boarded-up entrance. And then they were in – the three of them, huddled together in the damp blackness . . . ready to face two more of the hideous sailor dolls.

10

Cave Dwellers

The pencil torches threw out little light and it took quite a while for Billy and Calum to make out their surroundings.

They crawled along a small passage, until it opened out into a huge cavernous space, like a miniature cathedral. A large rock pool at the centre took up most of the floor space. The air was freezing cold. A strong smell of seaweed hung over everything and the sound of dripping water echoed ominously around the slimy walls.

'Can you see anything?' Calum whispered, nudging Billy as he crept around the edge of the rock pool.

'Not much. Just rocks and some smaller pools . . . and some bits of old wood lying around.'

The three of them crept slowly on, towards the back

of the 'cathedral'. Billy shone his torch down on a piece of half-rotted wood. He was just able to make out the faded letters: 'WHISKEY'.

'It's left over from the smuggled stuff I told you about,' Bunty said quietly, peering over his shoulder.

Calum took no notice. His voice began to shake. 'There's . . . there's . . . something up ahead . . . behind those rocks.'

Billy shone his torch forward so that his beam reinforced the light from Calum's. The backs of two small heads stuck out above a clump of rocks. The white sailor caps and wiry black hair left them in no doubt who the heads belonged to.

'They're not moving . . . they're lifeless!' Calum quaked.

'They'll only move when *he* wants them to,' Bunty said.

'But how does he do it?' Billy exclaimed. 'How can someone make dolls come alive?'

'Scullion isn't just "someone",' Bunty replied. 'He's an evil force capable of lots of things.'

'Lots of evil things, I suppose!' Billy whispered.

This time Bunty didn't reply. She remained very still and quiet. Billy swung round and shone his torch into her face. Her big green eyes stared back – but she wasn't looking at him. Her mind was elsewhere . . . like she was in some sort of trance.

'Is she OK?' Calum asked, his voice still shaking.

'I'm fine,' Bunty replied slowly. 'I can feel *his* presence . . . *he's* here.'

A cold draught of air appeared from nowhere. It whistled through the cave, making the hairs on Billy's neck stand on end. 'Same here,' Billy said. 'I can sense it too. And worse still . . . I can sense that he knows we're here!'

They all peered forward. Billy's torch lit up one of the heads as it turned slowly round and stared at them, its painted grin full of malice and its eyes cutting into them. They stood frozen as the other head did exactly the same.

'They're going to attack!' Bunty shrieked.

With torches in one hand and raised lengths of driftwood in the other, Billy and Calum braced themselves, but the heads disappeared down behind the rocks.

'They've gone!' Calum gasped.

Billy raised his weapon even higher and scanned around with his torch. 'No way! They're hiding . . . waiting to strike.'

A wave thundered just outside the cave entrance, followed by the sound of rushing water. At the same time, a sinister scuffling sounded from the other side of the cave. It filled Billy with terror . . . *and then the first doll struck.*

It leapt at Billy, but Calum got in the way. His cry echoed around the cave, only to be replaced by the sound of hideous demonic laughter.

'It's digging into me! Get it off!' Calum shrieked.

In the dark it was difficult to separate Calum from his attacker, but Billy managed to bring his weapon down hard, striking the top of the doll's head. He raised his weapon to deliver a second blow, but the wood was stuck . . . the rusty nails had buried into the wooden scalp.

Whilst Calum screamed, and Billy tried to free his weapon, Bunty delivered a second blow with her own piece of wood. Like Billy's, it stuck fast to the wooden doll and wouldn't move.

'Pull! Pull!' Billy shrieked, an idea forming in his mind.

He and Bunty pulled for all they were worth and the doll came free from Calum's waist, still attached by nails to their lumps of wood.

'Now chuck it in the pool!' Billy screamed.

Bunty understood.

In time with each other, they heaved their wooden weapons over the limestone ridge – complete with writhing doll – straight into the big rock pool.

A frantic splashing sounded from the other side of the rocks, and then all went quiet.

'I think it's climbed out!' Calum cried out, his voice full of panic.

Billy shone his torch into the stagnant seawater. His torch lit up the grinning lifeless face. 'No – it's floating . . .' Billy said, his voice trembling. 'I think it's finished.'

'Are you OK, Calum?' Billy asked.

'I'm scratched and bitten . . . but I'm OK.'

Another sinister scurrying noise reminded them that the battle wasn't over.

The tide roared again, waves crashing around the entrance.

'We're going to be trapped in here!' Billy murmured.

'And the other Dawn Demon's going to attack,' Bunty yelled at them. 'Follow me!'

'Where to?' Billy asked.

'Just follow me! I know another way out and I've got a plan.'

She scrambled past them towards the back of the cave. Billy and Calum chased after her. All the time they could hear the second dwarf-like figure creeping up behind them.

'This way!' Bunty ordered, beginning to climb upwards over a huge pile of fallen rocks. A ring of light began to show above their heads.

As they scrambled upwards, Bunty at the front and Billy at the rear, the circle of light grew bigger and brighter.

'We're almost there!' Bunty cried over her shoulder.

Billy stopped and shone his torch back down the rising tunnel. His blood froze as he saw the small face grinning up at him. It was moving fast . . . like a spider shooting up a web.

'QUICK . . . HE'S ALMOST GOT ME!' Billy shouted up to his two friends.

'We've made it!' Bunty sighed. She climbed out into the daylight on top of the cliff. Calum followed, but Billy couldn't move . . . the creature had grabbed his foot and was climbing up his leg. He screamed in terror. Calum reached down, grabbed Billy's arms and pulled for all he was worth.

'Get it off!' Billy shrieked.

With Calum's help, Billy dragged himself up the last few metres. He rolled out on to the grass, the Dawn Demon still clinging like a limpet to his leg.

'Get it off!' Billy screamed again. '*It's Hurting*!'

The doll's strength seemed unbelievable – Billy and Calum's combined efforts couldn't budge it. They needed Bunty's help . . . *but she'd disappeared*!

The doll bit into his leg. Billy shrieked. The doll laughed hideously and climbed further up his body.

A familiar voice suddenly bellowed out, ' "S" FOR "SCULLION" . . . "S" FOR "SCUM"!'

Billy swung around. Calum did the same. The doll let go of Billy's leg and rolled on to its back as Bunty appeared from behind a grass mound and towered over it. She held a large rock high above her head and she brought it down with all her strength.

A sickening sound of splintering wood marked the end of the battle.

With a look of pure hatred, Bunty kicked the mangled body back into the hole. She stood there with her hands on her hips and a big grin on her face, the lifeless remains cascading back down the narrow tunnel.

She turned to Billy and Calum and rubbed her hands. 'Three down, seven to go!'

Billy looked at Calum in disbelief. And then he studied his leg where his attacker had attached itself . . . it was red, some teeth marks, but the skin wasn't broken!

Calum pulled up his jumper and shirt. A series of claw marks stood out around his waist. One of them was deeper than the rest and bleeding a little. 'Those dolls are so strong,' he sighed.

'And they'll get stronger,' Bunty said.

Billy remembered his ear again. He rubbed his finger over it and felt the scab that had formed. 'How do you mean?'

'Bunty sat cross-legged on the grass by their side. 'Scullion's spirit is an evil force –'

'Nobody's arguing with that,' Calum chipped in.

Bunty frowned and carried on. 'He shared his power equally between his army of dolls.'

'Ten of them,' Calum said, already beginning to catch

on. Billy still wasn't sure what Bunty was leading up to.

'But now, thanks to us, there are only seven,' Bunty continued.

'So the rest of the dolls will have Scullion's power divided by seven,' Calum went on.

Billy couldn't understand the number side of it, but he began to see what Bunty and Calum were saying. 'And when there's only one doll left . . . then it will have all of Scullion's power . . . and be stronger than ever.'

'You've got it!' Calum said.

Billy climbed to his feet and dusted the grass off his trousers. 'So what next?'

'Go home and get some rest,' Bunty said. 'You're going to need it. I'll come and get you around dawn. Tomorrow morning we take on three more of them!'

Calum stood up and tucked his shirt in. 'And where will this next battle be?' he asked, his voice trembling a little – Billy wasn't sure whether it was from fear or excitement.

'I'll tell you when I see you . . . just go home, get some rest and get stuck into your Aunt Emily's steak and mushroom pie.'

Calum looked from Bunty to Billy and then back to Bunty again. 'But how do you know . . .? Oh forget it!'

Billy chuckled. Bunty was so cool. 'Why don't you come home with us? I'm sure there'll be enough for you. Aunt Emily won't mind.'

But Bunty was already walking away. As she disappeared around the grass mound, she shouted back over her shoulder. 'No thanks! I don't eat pies. In fact . . . *I don't eat at all*!'

11
Home Sweet Aunt Emily's

Billy felt so relieved to be back at Aunt Emily's. Everything seemed so safe and real again. He sat at the table and stared at the real tablecloth, the real china plates and the real cutlery. The smell of real steak and mushroom pie drifted in from the kitchen and Billy's mouth began to water.

'That smells so good,' Calum said, licking his lips.

Billy nodded. 'I wonder where Henry is.'

Calum glanced at the empty chair by the side of them. His place was set, but there was no sign of the old man. 'Don't know.'

Aunt Emily appeared with a huge shortcrust pie in a patterned dish that matched the plates. She placed it on a mat at the centre of the table and cut into it. 'I hope you two are hungry. Henry's not eating with us tonight. He's staying out at a friend's.'

Calum beamed. Billy beamed.

'Have you had a good day?' Aunt Emily continued. 'Did you get chance to look round the lifeboat station?'

As Aunt Emily served up the steaming pie and a mountain of potatoes and vegetables, Billy told her how they'd bumped into Henry and seen the photos of Uncle Jack in the station. He also told her about seeing the newspaper cutting describing the lifeboat disaster.

'It was the worst night of my life,' Aunt Emily said sadly. 'That boat cost my Jack his life. And all for the sake of those vile men . . . I can't help cursing the lot of them!'

Billy gave Aunt Emily a sad glance. He felt so sorry for her.

Calum frowned, but tried to keep the conversation going. 'You mean the smugglers?' he asked. 'Scullion's men?'

As the two boys began eating, Aunt Emily sat at the other end of the table, opposite Henry's place. 'There's not much gets past you two, that's for sure.'

'Henry mentioned Scullion to us,' Billy said.

Aunt Emily nodded solemnly. 'Henry couldn't stand the man. He blames him for everything that ever went wrong in this town . . . especially for the loss of that poor young girl and her mother.'

'What happened to them?' Calum asked, his mouth almost too full to speak.

Aunt Emily's expression turned to sadness. 'It happened years ago. They got into a mess and walked off the end of the pier – mother and daughter. The older folk in the town still talk about it. It doesn't bear thinking about!'

Billy and Calum stopped chewing and looked at each other – and then at Aunt Emily. She changed her face and forced a smile. 'Well that's enough of that . . . Get stuck in and I'll just get the salt.' And saying this she got up and disappeared into the kitchen.

'Are you thinking what I'm thinking?' Calum asked, his eyes still wide.

Billy's mind swirled with confused thoughts: Bunty and her mum . . . ghosts and mermaids . . . ends of piers . . . smugglers and sailor dolls . . .

He tried desperately to string it all together, but Calum began to do it for him.

'It's starting to make sense,' Calum began. 'First Scullion gets on the wrong side of just about everybody in Scawlsby – what with smuggling and lending out money that people can't afford to pay back. And then he drives a woman and her daughter to suicide.'

'And . . . you think Bunty is the girl – that went off the end of the pier?' Billy stammered.

Calum had just taken another mouthful of pie and

almost choked on it. 'No wonder she doesn't leave any footprints. She's a ghost!'

'But if Scullion is dead, why would he come back and wreck the town with sailor dolls?' Billy asked, suddenly losing interest in his food.

'The missing piece of the jigsaw,' Calum replied, still tucking into his food. 'And I think I know who might just have the answer,' he said mysteriously.

Billy looked at him thoughtfully. 'Who?'

Calum nodded at the empty chair by his side. 'Henry!'

Billy clapped his hands together. Calum was right. If anyone knew Scullion's motive, it would be Henry. He was an old, old man – about the right age to have been around at the time it all happened – and his eyes so hollow and full of sadness.

If anyone knew, Henry did.

After an evening watching TV and doing other normal things that normal people do, Billy suggested to Calum that they should get an early night, as they'd have to be up at dawn again. As they got ready for bed, they sneaked some antiseptic cream out of Aunt Emily's bathroom cabinet and treated their cuts and scratches.

Billy drifted into a restless sleep and his mind wandered away into a watery world.

He dreamt he was walking on the seabed again. Long trails of seaweed clung to his legs as he made his way towards the circle of dolphins. But this time the dolphins turned into sharks with long pointed snouts and razor teeth.

The predators swam around and around and finally parted to reveal the figure sitting at their centre – but not the beautiful mermaid as before. This time, a sinister skeleton in long flowing robes and wearing a crown!

The figure stared greedily at the treasure chest in front of it. The lid of the chest was slightly open and Billy saw bottles and cigarettes stashed inside. He drifted up to the chest and flung the lid fully open. And suddenly the chest revealed a grinning doll's face sneering up at him – a face full of hate and malice – and the doll swum out, followed by another and another.

And then Billy found himself surrounded by dozens of swimming sailor dolls, each baring their teeth and preparing to attack. The seated skeleton laughed at him, jeering and mocking, the hideous laughter growing louder with every second.

The seaweed clung tighter to Billy's legs, and the pain became unbearable. And when Billy finally looked down, he saw the hideous dolls clinging to each of his thighs, digging their wooden fingers into his flesh and grinning up at him . . .

And just as the nightmare reached its peak and Billy's brain felt it couldn't cope any more, a soft voice called from the distant watery depths: 'Billy . . . Billy . . . Follow me . . .'

He looked up and saw the mermaid, hazy in the distance – the familiar green eyes, the long blonde curls swaying in the current . . . the warm smile. And suddenly the dolls and the pain and all the nightmarish feelings were gone . . . just the soft, soothing voice beckoning him.

'Billy . . . Billy . . . Wake up!'

Billy opened his eyes and saw a shadow standing at the foot of his bed. He sat up and rubbed his eyes, unsure whether he was still dreaming.

Bunty seemed to read his mind. 'You're not dreaming. It's me – Bunty! I'm really here. Wake Calum up and meet me outside. I'll wait by the gate.'

Billy rubbed his eyes again and looked back. She was gone!

Calum stirred and turned towards him. 'What's up? What time is it?'

Billy looked at the bedside clock – 3.45 am. 'It's nearly dawn!'

Calum stirred again and looked up at him with half-closed eyes. 'Go back to sleep. She's never going to find us at this time.'

Billy pushed the duvet back and swung his legs out over the edge of the bed. 'She already has,' he said in a slightly shaky voice.

Calum sat up. 'Are you OK, Billy? You sound nervous . . . like you've seen a ghost.'

'I have!' Billy replied. 'She's waiting outside.'

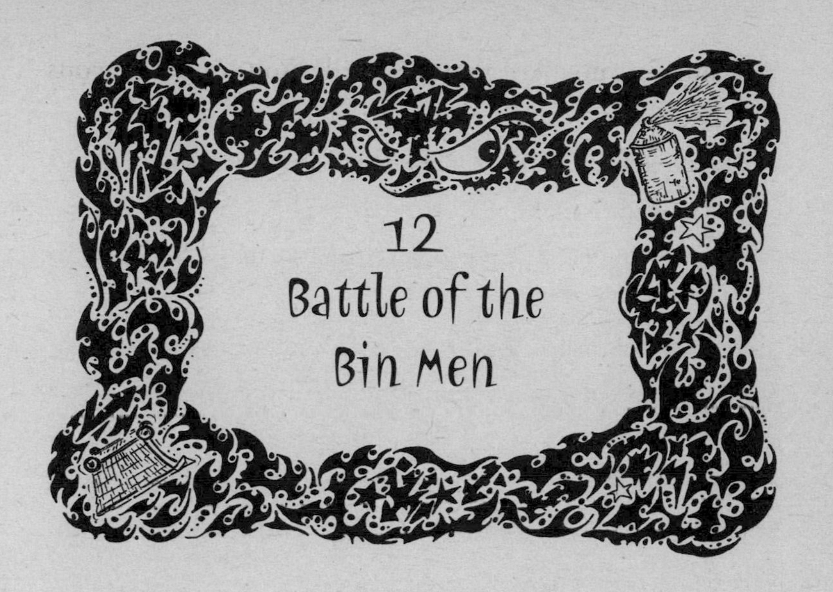

The streets were cold, dark and deserted. Bunty was waiting at the gate with a large dog beside her.

'Blimey! Where's he come from?' Calum asked.

'He followed me here. He's sweet,' Bunty said, looking down at the Alsatian. Billy walked up cautiously to the animal. It wagged its tail and panted enthusiastically. He leant down and stroked its head. 'No collar!'

'Must be a stray,' Calum suggested.

'Whoever he is, he's friendly,' Bunty said. 'He might even come in useful. Come on, boy! Let's go!'

The three children moved off, the dog following at a close distance.

As they turned the corner into Belper Street, Billy came straight out with the question that he and Calum had been waiting to ask their new friend. 'Bunty . . . are you a ghost?'

Bunty marched on and never even looked up. 'Yes, I suppose I am . . .'

Calum jogged a few steps to catch up with her. 'So you're not real?'

Bunty still didn't look up. 'I feel real enough when I'm with you – but not so real when I'm on my own . . . I suppose!'

Billy and Calum gawped at each other. 'So can you walk through walls and do all that ghost stuff?' Calum asked.

'Yes, most of the time.'

'Wow!' Calum gasped.

'Brilliant!' Billy added.

A thousand more questions flowed through Billy's mind, but before he or Calum could ask anything else, she stopped and put her finger to her lips.

The dog began to growl behind them.

'What's wrong, boy?' Billy whispered.

The dog's ears went back and the fur on its neck stood on end. It refused to move forward.

'Animals can sense evil faster than humans,' Bunty said in a matter-of-fact way.

Billy and Calum glanced ahead. They'd been so taken up in quizzing Bunty that they hadn't seen the alleyway looming up. 'We passed this alley on the way home from the pier,' Billy said. 'I saw something moving about in the shadows.'

'And we found some interesting graffiti the next day,' Calum added.

The dog began to whine and walk backwards.

'I'm not surprised,' Bunty said seriously. 'It's a bad place at night. We need to be very careful. Follow me.'

Bunty edged along the wall up to the entrance to the alleyway. Billy and Calum followed her example. The dog stayed well back, half whining and half growling. Bunty peered around the corner. Billy and Calum crouched beside her and did the same.

The alleyway was in darkness, but it was easy to pick out the silhouettes of the three wheely bins standing among the shadows. A deathly silence hung over everything. Billy became aware of goosebumps breaking out across his body.

'They're in the bins,' Bunty whispered. 'Waiting for him to send them out.'

'Scullion?' Calum whispered.

Bunty nodded.

'To do his dirty work!' Billy added.

Bunty nodded again.

'How do we fight them this time?' Billy asked nervously.

Bunty fumbled in the pouch on the front of her kilt. She took out two small cans, each with a plastic nozzle, and a box of matches. 'With these!' she whispered.

She passed one of the cans to Billy and the other to Calum. And then she reached into her pouch again and took out the pencil torches. The boys shone their mini torches on to the sides of the cans and read the lettering: 'LIGHTER FUEL'.

'Mum uses this in her cigarette lighter,' Billy said. 'It's highly inflan . . . inflammm . . .'

'Inflammable!' Calum finished for him.

'We need to move quick,' Bunty said impatiently. 'Before he brings them to life.'

Calum began to whisper in a high-pitched voice full of panic. 'You mean we've got to go up there and open those wheely bins and . . .'

'Exactly!' Bunty said firmly.

'It's too late!' Billy gasped.

They gazed up the alleyway and watched in horror as one of the wheely-bin lids lifted slowly and purposefully into the air. A second one quickly followed and then a third.

'Blimey! They're coming out!' Calum croaked.

The dog began to growl more loudly behind them.

'We'll have to retreat!' Bunty said. 'Across the road and behind that parked car . . . We'll hide there and decide what to do next.'

Nobody wanted to argue with that. They quickly turned on their heels and crept across the road. They gestured to the dog to follow them, and a few seconds later they were all peering from behind a parked car over to the alleyway.

The hairs on the back of Billy's neck stood on end as three dwarf-like figures emerged from the dark passage and stalked away up Belper Street. The hideous sound of high-pitched chuckling trailed away into the distance as the figures disappeared.

'Now what do we do?' Calum whispered.

'We set a trap for when they get back,' Bunty answered.

'How?'

'I don't know. Any ideas?'

'I've got one,' Billy said. 'We'll need to act fast.'

Billy led them back across the road and up the alleyway. The three wheely bins stood with their lids open, waiting for the return of their occupants. Billy peered into them and saw that each one was about half full of paper and rubbish – no doubt a cosy bed for their daytime occupants.

'What's the plan?' Bunty asked.

'Trust me!' Billy replied. 'Pass me the lighter fuel.'

Bunty and Calum watched as Billy sprayed the contents of the cans into each of the three wheely bins.

'OK, let's get back across the road . . .'

Back behind the parked car, they crouched down and Billy began taking one of his socks off.

'What are you doing now?' Calum asked.

Billy pointed behind to a rose bush sprouting over the garden wall. 'See that garden cane? Pass it here . . . and see if you can find a couple more.'

Bunty stroked the top of the dog's head and gave Billy a strange look as he took his other sock off.

The dog started to growl again. Bunty looked anxiously across the road. 'Watch out! They're back!' she whispered.

The three friends kept low as the leading doll stopped under a lamppost just short of the alleyway. The other two figures watched as it climbed up the post and put its fist through the glass light. A horrible high-pitched chuckling followed.

'Calum, I need one of your socks . . . quick!'

Calum didn't argue. He kicked one of his shoes off and removed his sock.

Billy sat with his back to the garden wall and wrapped each of the three socks around the end of a garden cane. Then he doused each sock with some lighter fuel he'd saved in one of the cans.

They all watched as the shadowy figures crept back up the alleyway, and Billy guessed that they were ready to return to their hiding places.

'Take one of these,' he said, passing Bunty and Calum a cane each, complete with sock soaked in lighter fuel. 'Now follow me!'

They crept over the road. The dog refused to move and stayed hidden.

Crouching by the entrance to the alleyway, they saw the distant silhouettes scrambling back into the bins.

'OK!' Billy whispered. 'I'm going to light our torches.'

Keeping well out of sight, he struck a match and held it to the socks. Bunty and Calum held their blazing torches and waited for Billy's command.

His voice shook with excitement. 'There's no time to waste. Just dash up the alleyway, open one of the bins and drop the torch in.'

Calum stammered and stuttered. 'But . . . but . . .'

Bunty didn't hesitate. She charged around the corner, sprinted up to the nearest wheely bin and did exactly as Billy said. Billy did the same. Calum took a deep breath and followed their example.

The result was dramatic.

The fuel-doused rubbish ignited and burst into flame. Within seconds, each of the bins became a blazing inferno. Billy, Calum and Bunty retreated down the alleyway and turned to face the spectacle. Through the flames it was just possible to see each of the three dwarf-like figures trying desperately to escape from their hideout. Two of the figures fell back into the blazing bins. But the third doll managed to drop to the ground, still on fire. It rolled on the floor and made a hideous screeching sound until the flames were extinguished. Blackened and charred, it got to its feet and faced down the alleyway.

'Watch out!' Billy exclaimed. 'It's going to charge!'

The doll proved Billy correct as it sprinted towards them at lightning speed. It struck Billy's stomach with such force that it drove him five metres back into the middle of the road and flattened him.

Bunty and Calum, who so far had remained shocked and speechless, sprang into action.

'Get it off him!' Calum shrieked.

Billy looked up, dazed and groggy, as the smoking, blackened doll reared its ugly head and stared him straight in the eye. Never had he seen such a look of hatred and malice.

The doll grabbed Billy's neck and shrieked and snarled. And then it leant over him and opened its thick wooden lips, baring its charred teeth . . .

Bunty and Calum dashed to Billy's aid . . . but the dog beat them to it. It charged from across the road and hit the doll with terrific force. It sank its sharp canine teeth into its neck and carried it away up the road.

Bunty cheered as the dog shook the doll violently. The legs still smoked as the bottom half of its body separated from its head and shoulders . . . and then it was all over – the doll was no more than a lifeless pile of wood!

'STAY THERE . . . BLOOMING VANDALS!' A

woman had appeared on the doorstep of number seventeen. She stood in dressing gown and slippers and had her arms folded across her chest.

Several other lights came on and a siren sounded somewhere in the distance.

'Quick . . . we need to get out of here!' Bunty screamed.

It was only a short sprint back to Gladstone Terrace. They charged through the gate and hid in Aunt Emily's garden. They watched as a fire engine roared past, followed closely by a police car . . . and an ambulance.

'Someone must have dialled 999,' Calum said quietly.

'Billy . . . your plan was fab,' Bunty whispered.

'A bit risky though,' Calum added.

Billy nodded. 'Well, at least it worked, and that's three less Dawn Demons to worry about.'

Their hearts all skipped a beat as a heavy panting sounded from the other side of the privet hedge. Calum, being the tallest, peered over first. 'Phew! It's the dog,' he sighed. 'And look what it's carrying.'

They all peered over and watched as the Alsatian dropped something at its feet and stared up at them.

'It's the sailor doll – or what's left of it. Good boy!' Billy said.

Bunty got up, put her hands on her hips and turned to face them. 'I'll see you soon.' She looked down at Billy and smiled warmly at him. 'Six down and four to go!'

Billy and Calum said nothing. They scrambled to their feet and watched as Bunty moved through the gate with the dog following after her.

She disappeared down the street and never looked back.

But Billy sensed it would only be a short time before they met up again.

13 Ghostly Warnings

The two boys sneaked in the back door and Billy made sure he dropped the latch on the lock! They crept upstairs and hoped they hadn't been missed. The sound of gentle snoring from Aunt Emily's room, and loud snoring from old Henry next door, reassured them that they hadn't.

Five minutes later they were back in bed, Calum whispering fervently, going over and over the recent events. Billy hardly heard a word, he was so tired. What a weird night! Or was it morning? He craved sleep.

However, as usual, Calum was asleep before him, breathing deeply by his side. And just as Billy's own eyes began to close, something disturbed him. It was a sound from downstairs. He strained his ears. There it was again . . . footsteps . . . definitely footsteps.

Someone was moving about down below.

He crept out of bed and moved towards the landing. He was tempted to wake Calum, but decided against it. Perhaps Henry had got out of bed and was wandering about. But no! Billy could still hear the old man snoring from his bedroom.

Taking one step at a time and treading lightly, Billy made his way down the stairs. He stood at the bottom and listened, hoping that the sound would go away. But it didn't! He heard footsteps again . . . but more distant now . . . from the kitchen.

He picked up the poker from the side of the fire and raised it to his shoulder. With his heart beating ever faster, he peered around the kitchen door and prepared for the worst.

There was no one there!

He sighed with relief. And then heard more footsteps . . . from the other side of the cellar door . . . *which was open*!

Something was definitely moving down the stone steps leading to the cellar. Billy crept towards the open door, but decided that no way was he going down there. With his heart in his mouth, he peered down the steps. All was in darkness. But to his horror, he was able to make out the outline of a tall figure standing at the bottom of the steps.

'Come on down, Billy,' a gentle voice called up to

him. 'I'm not going to hurt you.' There was real warmth in the voice.

'Can I put the light on?'

'Course you can, lad. Come on down. I want a word.'

Billy flicked the light switch on and stared down the steps. The figure was gone! This was getting frustrating!

'Are you still down there?' Billy called as loudly as he dared. He didn't want to disturb anyone else in the house.

'Still here, Billy. I'm resting my legs around the corner. You needn't be afraid. Come on down . . . I promise I won't bite.'

Despite his instincts telling him that the figure was friendly, Billy raised his weapon again – just to be on the safe side – and started down the steps. As he neared the bottom, a strong smell of seaweed filled his nostrils.

This is getting weirder and weirder, Billy thought to himself.

He raised his weapon higher, took a deep breath and darted around the corner into the main cellar.

'I wonder what your Aunt Emily would say if she saw you with her poker,' the seaman laughed – at least he looked like a seaman.

Billy stared in awe at the figure seated in front of him. The man wore a yellow oilskin coat over black trousers and big Wellington boots.

'Come and sit by me, Billy,' the man said kindly. He

pulled up a wooden box and gestured Billy to sit on it.

'Who are you?' Billy asked, starting to relax a little.

'Your Uncle Jack.'

Billy sat down and looked into the man's face. His eyes were blue – as blue as any ocean Billy had ever seen. What with his curly black hair, bronzed skin and flashing white teeth, he reminded Billy of a handsome pirate . . . a film star. 'Well, you do look like the photographs – *but you're dead*!' Billy said. And then he thought better of it, 'Sorry! I didn't mean to sound . . .'

The man laughed and clapped his hands together. 'Don't apologize, lad. You're right – I'm as dead as a doormail!'

Billy looked into the kind face again. It was definitely Uncle Jack! 'So you must be a ghost!'

'Aye . . . like the girl you and your pal hang around with.'

'Bunty?'

'Aye, that's right. Bunty Watkins. She's the reason I'm here.'

Billy tensed. He sensed there was some bad news on the way. Uncle Jack leant forward and placed his big hands on his knees. 'Bunty means well. She's a heart of gold . . . like you lad!'

Billy felt the colour rush into his cheeks. 'So what's the problem?'

Uncle Jack leant even closer and the smell of seaweed

made Billy feel nauseous. 'The problem is that she'll stop at nothing until all them sailor dolls are done for and Scullion is back where he belongs . . .'

Billy fidgeted nervously on his box. 'Where does he belong?'

The expression on Uncle Jack's face turned serious. He looked above Billy's head and stared into space. 'With the Devil, son!' He looked at Billy again. 'It was his greed that drove Bunty and her mother to finish up the way they did – but I think you already know that . . . just like you know all about those sailor dolls.'

Billy nodded. 'You mean the Dawn Demons?'

'Is that what you call 'em?'

Billy nodded. 'Bunty told us . . . it's what she calls them.'

'Well, as I was saying, that young lass will stop at nothing until they're all done for. Even if it means putting you at risk . . . and that pal of yours.'

'But we like Bunty!' Billy said defensively. 'She wouldn't do anything to hurt us.'

Uncle Jack frowned and stared hard into Billy's eyes. 'No, I know that. But Scullion won't stop until he's brought this town to its knees. That's his plan, you see, and you've interfered. Bunty's got you and your mate involved.'

'And we're winning!' Billy beamed.

'Six down and four to go, eh?' Uncle Jack smiled, but

still with a stern look in his eyes. 'And you know that every time you get rid of one, the others get stronger?'

Billy nodded. Uncle Jack seemed to know everything. 'Yes, Bunty told us. And she knows where they all are.'

'And no doubt the three of you are going to hunt them down and finish them off and put paid to Scullion's plans forever!'

'That's the idea!' Billy said proudly, but with a hint of nervousness in his voice.

Uncle Jack smiled kindly again. 'Look, Billy. That's why I'm here – to warn you. Scullion knows you're on to him and that you mean business. Those dolls of his – "Dawn Demons" or whatever you want to call them – they're not going to sit tight and wait for you and your mates to find them.'

Billy's voice trembled a little more. 'What do you mean?'

'Scullion will have them strike you first, so you'd better be on your guard, lad. Bunty may be a gutsy lass – she's a strong spirit – but she's no match for Scullion. He's the Devil's own!'

Billy felt the familiar butterflies fluttering in his stomach. The seaman was right. They'd already suffered one unprovoked attack on the ghost train. He looked into Uncle Jack's face again and decided it was the most caring face he'd ever seen.

'What's it like to be dead?' Billy suddenly asked.

'Sometimes it's better than being alive, son . . . but I miss your Aunt Emily – and especially her homemade steak and mushroom pies.' Billy's uncle laughed. 'I don't suppose you saved me any?'

Billy smiled and wished his uncle had survived that horrible storm. He would have been the best uncle ever.

'I've got to go, son,' Uncle Jack said, climbing to his feet. 'Now, remember what I said. Be on your guard day and night. And don't rely too much on Bunty. You need to take charge now, Billy. You're a special lad . . . they don't come much cleverer than you!'

Billy nodded solemnly.

'And one final thing,' the sailor said, rising to his feet. 'Always remember the old saying: "*Red sky at night . . . shepherds' delight. Red sky dawning . . . sailors' warning*".'

Billy looked puzzled. 'But what does that mean, exactly?'

A familiar voice cut him off. It sounded from the top of the cellar steps. 'Is that you, Billy?'

Billy ran to the bottom of the cellar steps and looked up. Aunt Emily was standing there in her dressing gown and slippers.

'Whatever are you doing down there at this hour?' she whispered.

Billy wasn't even sure what hour it was. 'Sorry! But you'll never believe who I'm talking to. Come and have a look!' His heart raced with excitement at the thought of Aunt Emily seeing Uncle Jack again.

Aunt Emily frowned and walked quickly down the steps to join him. He led her around the corner and pointed excitedly towards the two upturned boxes . . . *nobody there*!

Billy dragged Aunt Emily over to where he and his uncle had sat. 'He was here, Aunt Emily. I promise you. It was Uncle –'

'That's enough, young man!' Aunt Emily interrupted. 'You've been dreaming again – sleepwalking – and it's time you were back in bed. It's almost time to get up!'

It was obvious to Billy that Aunt Emily didn't want to hear any more.

As they turned to leave, he noticed a small puddle of slimy green water where Uncle Jack's boots had rested on the floor. He also noticed the faint smell of seaweed still hanging in the air.

But most of all, he noticed a tear in Aunt Emily's eye as she took his arm and led him away back to bed.

14
Surprise Attack

The next morning, while they were getting dressed, Billy told Calum about his early-morning encounter in the cellar. During breakfast, they continued their conversation in low whispers to avoid Henry hearing them. The old man slurped his cereal and eyed them with suspicion.

'It's rude to whisper!' Aunt Emily said, bustling in with a plate of toast. 'What are you two planning to do today?'

'Not sure yet,' Billy said. 'We're just discussing it.'

'Well, you could do a bit of shopping for me. I'm out of shampoo and loo paper and I could do with a few other things.'

Billy nodded in Calum's direction. Calum nodded back.

'OK. We'll have a look around the shops this morning and maybe have a walk on the beach this afternoon.'

'It's all right for some!' Henry muttered, loud enough for them to hear. 'I've got work to do.'

Aunt Emily collected his empty cereal bowl and scoffed at him. 'And you love every minute of it down on that allotment. So don't be an old moaner!'

Henry pretended not to hear and reached for a piece of toast. Billy and Calum did the same.

'What's an allotment?' Billy whispered.

'It's a kind of garden where old people grow potatoes and stuff,' Calum answered.

'Not just old people and not just potatoes,' Henry muttered. 'You should come up and have a look. You could even make yourself useful and give me a hand for an hour. It might toughen you up a bit.'

Billy always liked to make himself useful. 'Where is it?' he asked.

'Five minutes away . . . other end of Alderman Street.'

Billy looked at Calum. He was chewing a mouthful of toast. 'We could go up this afternoon instead of going on the beach.' Calum nodded. 'We'll come and find you this afternoon then,' Billy said, smiling at the old man.

'I'll believe it when I see it,' Henry said, getting up to leave the table.

Aunt Emily came in from the kitchen again. 'I've made

you a list. There's not much. And before I forget, would you both give your mums a ring, just to let them know you're fine.'

'OK!' Billy and Calum replied at the same time.

An hour later, the two boys were walking up the high street. Unlike the rest of the town, the main shopping precinct looked quite new and fresh. The shop windows were filled with brightly-coloured posters and attractive displays, and everywhere seemed busy.

'Fancy a look in here?' Calum asked, peering into a window full of computer games and DVDs. Billy nodded.

A few minutes later, they were back in the street. Calum beamed at Billy, delighted with his new purchase, a computer game called Zombie Warriors!

'It's a pity Aunt Emily's not got a PC,' Billy sighed.

'No big deal!' Calum replied cheerily. 'It'll wait till we get home.'

He took the game out of the bag and examined the bright packaging, before passing it to Billy.

Billy looked at it admiringly. 'Brilliant!'

Before either of them had time to say anything else, Billy felt a hard knock on the back of his left knee. He turned and looked down as a small hooded figure reached up and snatched the computer game from his hand.

'Hey!' he screamed instinctively.

But the figure had already hared off up the busy street and disappeared among the shoppers.

'Get after him!' Calum yelled.

Billy had already set off in chase, weaving his way through the shoppers, desperate to catch sight of the small hooded thief. 'I CAN SEE HIM!' Billy yelled back to Calum. 'He's gone round that corner!'

Calum managed to catch Billy up and a moment later they found themselves running up a narrow passageway between two stores. 'THERE HE GOES!' Calum shouted.

They raced on through a network of narrow alleyways between the backs of the shops, the small hooded figure just managing to keep ahead of them. The final passage opened out on to a square area of waste ground enclosed by high walls. They were just in time to see the thief disappear behind a large waste skip. An abandoned pram stood in front of it.

There was no one around and the enclosed area suddenly seemed very lonely. Billy began to feel threatened and vulnerable. They moved on towards the pram.

'Stop!' Billy said sternly, pulling at Calum's arm.

'What's wrong?'

'I don't like it!'

'Like what?'

Billy stared nervously ahead.

The pram . . . the waste skip full of rubbish . . . several abandoned supermarket trolleys . . . high brick walls covered in graffiti . . . old cans, chip cartons and other litter scattered on the ground – the scene made him feel uncomfortable. 'There's something not right! You stay here and watch my back.'

'Blimey! This is like one of those films you see on TV,' Calum joked. But Billy sensed that his friend was putting on an act. Calum was really just as scared as he was.

Billy walked towards the abandoned pram and an eerie silence descended over everything. To make matters worse, the sky grew darker as black clouds gathered overhead. It began to spit with rain.

Billy reached the old pram, grabbed the chrome handle, and tipped it towards him so he could see inside. The sight of the back of the baby's head almost caused his heart to stop.

'What's wrong?' Calum shouted nervously.

'There's a baby inside!'

'I can't believe it,' Calum shouted.

Billy leant closer and peered in at the baby's head. It was almost hidden under the blankets. And then, all at once, it stirred and turned to face him. Billy shrieked in terror as the evil face glared up at him.

'IT'S ONE OF THEM!' Billy yelled.

As he jumped back, the doll thrust out its clawing hands and grabbed hold of his hair. He stumbled backwards and fell flat on his back, the doll still clinging to his head and sitting astride his neck.

Calum ran to his rescue, but stopped in his tracks as the small figure in the black duffle coat appeared on top of the rubbish skip. It dropped its hood and started laughing hysterically – high-pitched devilish laughter!'

'We've been tricked!' Calum gasped.

But Billy had too much on his mind to take any notice. The doll knelt on his chest, its painted wooden hands squeezing his neck with incredible strength.

As the second doll leapt down from the rubbish skip and hurled it'self at Calum, Billy coughed and choked and struggled for breath. He pushed and pushed at the hideous little face, but it wouldn't budge . . . it just kept on squeezing. It was only as he stretched his left arm out that he felt the brick by his side. He grasped it and smashed it into the doll's face. The brick was heavy; it knocked the doll off his chest like a bowling ball toppling a skittle.

Meanwhile, the second Dawn Demon hurled itself at Calum and latched on to his knee, clawing and biting at his leg. Calum screamed and punched its hard wooden head.

At the same time, the first doll sprang back to its feet and faced Billy, ready to resume its attack . . .

until a metallic ringing sound distracted it.

They all swung round as the girl charged forward, pushing the supermarket trolley. It bumped, clanged and gathered momentum, on course for the doll standing at Billy's feet.

Billy's attacker stood frozen, unsure what to do . . . until it was too late!

The trolley rolled over the doll and knocked it to the floor, entangling it between the wheels and the trolley bottom. Billy needed no telling what to do. He jumped to his feet and leapt into the trolley, his added weight helping pin the doll to the ground.

Meanwhile, the second doll detached itself from Calum's leg, pulled up its hood and charged back towards the rubbish skip, disappearing around the back of it.

While the doll squirmed beneath the trolley, Bunty picked up the brick that Billy had thrown earlier.

'OK, Billy, when I count to three, jump out,' Bunty said, raising the brick ready to strike.

Billy did as she said. On the count of three, he leapt out of the trolley and the doll tried to free itself. But Bunty was far too quick. She brought the brick down on to the doll's head, splitting it in two.

Billy fell back into a sitting position on the hard ground. His neck really hurt. He stared at the smashed doll lying close to his feet and saw that parts of it were still twitching. 'Scullion's still trying to control it,' he croaked.

Bunty picked up the brick. She brought it down on the prostrate doll again and again, smashing it to pieces. 'It's not moving now!' she said triumphantly.

As Calum tended to his wounds, Billy stared up at Bunty as she towered over her victim, an expression of grim determination written all over her face.

Uncle Jack had been exactly right. Bunty was determined to beat Scullion and his vile army – and Billy was part of that battle, and Calum too. But this time the Dawn Demons had been one step ahead of them and had tricked them, and Bunty had only just managed to save them.

What about next time?

He and Calum would need all their senses to be on full alert. Bunty might not always be there.

She came over, held out her hand and pulled him up with amazing strength.

'Another one done for,' she said proudly. 'Seven down and three to go.'

Billy watched as Calum climbed to his feet and walked over towards the rubbish skip. He picked up the computer game lying abandoned on the floor. He tried to dust it down and began fiddling with it. Billy saw the look of despair on his face. 'Oh well, I suppose three's not too many . . .' he said, trying to sound encouraging.

But in his head, Billy was thinking that three dolls were still a lot of dolls – and his aching neck only confirmed what Bunty had said from the beginning: *the Dawn Demons were getting stronger all the time*!

15
Detective Inspector Prior

Aunt Emily's shopping had finally been remembered and dropped off at the house. And now the rain began to fall in torrents as Bunty ran on towards Alderman Street, with Billy and Calum trying desperately to keep up.

'Blimey . . . are we nearly there?' Calum gasped.

'He said the allotments were only five minutes away,' Billy replied, his throat still feeling sore from the doll attack.

Bunty stopped and called back to them. 'Nearly there . . . Keep up – you'll get soaked.'

The raindrops turned to silver rods and pummelled into the pavement. 'We can't get any wetter!' Billy cried through the watery veil. 'How about you?'

'I'm soaked to the skin,' Bunty yelled in a cheery voice, 'but I love it! I'm a mermaid, remember?'

Calum looked across to Billy and shrugged his shoulders.

A few minutes later, which seemed like an eternity, they reached a fence made up from corrugated sheeting. The sheets were covered in graffiti and one of the tags brought a sharp reaction from Calum and Billy.

'Look! The wheely bin with the eyes peeping out! The Dawn Demons have been here,' Calum said.

'They've been here all right,' Bunty sighed. 'The gate's smashed in.'

Billy looked from the brightly-daubed image to the wooden door in the fence. It was hanging off its hinges and had a hole punched through the middle.

Bunty shoved the door to one side and entered the allotments. 'I don't know where the old man hangs out,' Bunty said. 'We'll have to take a look. He shouldn't be hard to find . . . if he's still here!'

'Let's hope he's OK,' Billy said. 'I can see a shed with smoke coming out of a chimney. It could be him sheltering inside.'

'I hope so,' Calum sighed. 'I've had enough of this! I'm soaked!'

'Look! Some of the plants have been pulled up,' Bunty said. 'Dawn Demons again!'

Billy glanced around the rectangular garden plots. Even through the rain it was easy to spot the rows of winter vegetables pulled up and strewn across the ground.

'I hope old Henry's safe!' Billy repeated.

A nervous look spread across Calum's face. 'Do you think those devil dolls could still be around?'

Bunty shook her head. 'I don't think so. It all looks quiet to me. And it's raining too hard – even for the Dawn Demons!' She headed back towards the wrecked gate.

Billy and Calum glanced at each other. 'Where are you going?' they asked together.

Bunty grinned. 'Back to the bottom of the sea . . . where nobody worries about getting wet. Catch you later!'

And she was gone.

'That girl can be so frustrating,' Calum fumed.

And so useful, Billy thought to himself. He felt much more vulnerable when she wasn't around. 'Let's check out that hut!'

They ran on through a patchwork of garden plots heading towards a shed with a crooked metal chimney, a thin column of smoke rising from it. Billy knocked on the door and hoped that it would open to reveal a familiar face.

'GO AWAY!' a gruff voice boomed from inside.

Billy looked at Calum. The rain dripped off their hair and ran down their necks. 'It's us – Billy and Calum! We said we'd meet you here!' Billy shouted back.

There was a pause . . . a silence . . . just the sound of

the rain driving into the ground . . . followed by footsteps from inside the shed . . . cautious footsteps.

The door opened a little and a familiar face peered round at them. 'Good grief! I didn't expect you two to show up in this lot!'

Never had Billy been so pleased to see Henry. He could already feel the warmth and dryness from the other side of the door. By the look on Calum's face, he felt exactly the same.

'Don't just stand there! Come on in!' the old man ordered them. As soon as they were inside, he glanced outside, shut the door and locked it.

Meanwhile, the two boys gazed around their warm refuge.

An old stove stood in a corner. It had a small glass door, which was open. The bright-yellow flames presented a cheerful contrast to the foul weather outside. A small rug and an old armchair stood in front of it. A little table, a rickety old dining chair and a shabby chest of drawers were the only other items of furniture.

But it was the walls of the shed that commanded most of Billy and Calum's attention. They were covered in photographs and pictures, hardly a square inch of wood showing through them.

'Wow! Get a load of this!' Billy gasped.

'That's some collection! There's more pictures here than we saw at the lifeboat station,' Calum pointed out.

'Don't stand there dripping!' Henry mumbled at them. 'Get those coats off and I'll hang them by the stove. Did you see anything out there?'

'We saw the graffiti and the smashed gate,' Billy said.

'And some vegetables pulled up,' Calum added.

'Winter cabbage and sprouts!' Henry frowned.

They handed him their wet coats and the old man took them without speaking. Billy and Calum looked closely at the photographs.

'They're all policemen,' Calum said.

Billy looked from one photograph to another. Calum was right – lots of policemen, all standing in lines and looking serious. Some of the photographs looked much older than others . . . faded and yellow . . . their corners curling up.

'Scawlsby and District Constabulary,' Henry muttered from over by the stove. 'There are some more recent ones on that other wall.'

The two boys walked over to where Henry was pointing, and looked at the pictures. One of them showed a man in a smart suit, standing on his own.

'This is you!' Billy said in an excited voice.

Calum stood by him and scanned the photos eagerly. 'And these others . . . they're you as well – when you were younger.'

The old man sauntered over. 'You mean when I had more hair!'

Calum glanced at Billy. Billy smiled back at him. They went on studying the photographs.

'Wow! You were a detective inspector!' Calum said admiringly.

'I was . . . for ten years,' Henry said, cheering up a little.

'Detective Inspector Prior,' Billy said. 'Sounds brilliant!'

The old man's eyes sparkled. 'Come and sit on the rug – warm yourselves. There's something I want to show you.'

They did as Henry said and sat in front of the stove. The rain drummed rhythmically on the shed window and reminded them of the foul weather outside. They watched as the old man rummaged through a drawer and took out a pair of handcuffs.

'Wow! Are those handcuffs real?' Billy asked.

'Course they're real!' Henry replied. 'And still as good as new. You can look at them if you like.'

He threw them across the room. Billy caught them and stared at them admiringly. The metal glistened. 'Did you use these on real criminals?' he asked.

Henry looked disinterested. He was still rummaging through the drawer. 'Yes, lots of times. You can borrow them for a few days if you like. You'd better have the key.' He passed a small key across to Billy. 'Don't lose it!'

'Wow . . . lucky!' Calum said enviously.

Billy put the key in his pocket and began playing with

the handcuffs. They were so shiny. 'Brilliant!'

Henry seemed to find what he was looking for. He walked over, sat in the armchair and passed some more photographs to Calum and Billy. 'Put those handcuffs away and take a look at these,' he said, his expression very serious.

Billy looked at the top photograph. It showed a man's head and shoulders and a number written across the bottom. 'He looks mean!'

'Really mean!' Calum added. 'These photos are all of the same man, aren't they?'

Henry nodded. 'That's Scullion – the man I told you about. A nasty piece of work!'

Billy glanced over Calum's shoulder. 'What's the number written at the bottom?'

'His prison number,' Henry replied.

'So you got him in the end,' Calum stated, rather than asked.

The old man nodded solemnly. He got up from his chair and put some more wood on the stove. 'Yes – eventually! He was a thief, a smuggler and a loan shark.'

'What's a loan shark?' Billy asked.

'Someone who loans you money and then charges you twice as much when you have to pay it back,' Henry said.

'And then they get nasty when you can't afford it,' Calum added.

Henry nodded. 'That's right. And Scullion was really

nasty. He preyed on the weak – made their lives miserable . . . like Bunty's mum.'

'So why did people put up with him?' Billy asked.

'There were lots of desperate people in those days, and more than enough witnesses. But nobody dare speak up – the whole town was scared of him. But as you say, we got him in the end. He got twenty years. I was the arresting officer. We picked him up on the night of the storm – when your uncle got killed. He said he was innocent, of course, that he knew nothing about the drugs and other goods stashed onboard.'

Billy studied Scullion's photograph. His face was scary to say the least – fat and round with evil piggy eyes. His mouth was the worst – thick rubbery lips set in a scowl; crooked teeth, some of them black. 'So how come you managed to lock him up?'

The old man stared at the stove and gazed at the lively yellow flames. 'I finally persuaded folk to speak out . . . to give evidence. I told them the town would be a safer place without him.'

'And was it?' Billy asked.

Henry turned towards Billy and looked at him with big soulful eyes. 'It was . . . until he escaped.'

'Wow! How did he do that?' Billy and Calum asked together.

Henry hesitated . . . put his hands on his knees. '*He died . . .*'

The wood on the fire suddenly hissed and spat, the flames danced more brightly, and an eerie silence fell over the shed.

The old man finally continued. 'He died in prison not long ago . . . that's when the trouble started – the acts of vandalism, my house burning down.'

Calum gawped at Billy. Billy gawped back.

'So you know about Scullion's spirit . . . ghost . . . or whatever you want to call it?' Billy asked.

Henry nodded. 'And I know about the sailor dolls . . . and the young lass.'

'Bunty?' Calum said. 'You know about Bunty?'

'I know more than you think, lad,' Henry frowned, still nodding his head. 'Don't forget I was a policeman for most of my life.'

'A detective inspector . . .' Billy added.

Henry went back to the chest of drawers and took out a notebook. It looked old and well worn with all the corners dog-eared. 'I've been keeping a record of everything. I've even stayed up all night and watched out for those doll creatures.'

'Dawn Demons,' Billy said. 'That's what Bunty calls them.'

'And did you ever see them?' Calum asked.

Henry tapped his notebook. 'It's all in here, lad. I've seen them more than once.'

'So why didn't you tell the police?' Billy asked. 'Surely

they would have believed you – an ex-detective inspector.'

'And your house being burnt down – that's really serious,' Calum pointed out. 'You could have been killed.'

'It's called "arson", son. And you're right – it is a really serious crime. But do you think anyone in their right mind would have believed me when I told them I was a victim of a gang of sailor dolls . . . controlled by a dead man?'

'Suppose not!' Billy agreed.

'The ravings of an old man – that's what they would have said. I would have agreed with them when I was younger.'

A gust of wind rattled the window. Billy moved closer to the stove. 'It's really cosy and warm in here,' he said.

Henry sat back in his armchair, Billy and Calum by his feet. 'This is my second home. I love it here,' the old man sighed. 'Now they've even spoilt that. Nowhere's safe with those . . . Dawn whatsits around. Scullion won't rest till the town's as dead as he is – and me as well! I still remember the day he was sent down . . . shouting and screaming. He swore he'd get his revenge on the townsfolk for putting him behind bars.'

This was it! The missing piece of the jigsaw! Calum had guessed that Henry would know Scullion's motives for all the trouble – and he'd been right!

Billy looked back to Henry and felt sorry for him. No wonder the old man had seemed miserable and grumpy. Scullion and his Devil Army were making life impossible for him. 'We'll try and help you,' Billy said enthusiastically.

Calum nodded. 'We'll do everything we can.'

Henry turned his head towards them and managed a feeble smile.

A sudden thumping sound from the roof caused them all to look upwards.

'God . . . what was that?' Calum stammered.

The old man almost jumped out of his chair. He made his way over to the window and peered out – the raindrops were still streaming down the glass.

'Can . . . can you see anything?' Calum asked with a worried look on his face.

'No, son . . . I can't see anything. But that's no pigeon on the roof!'

More loud bangs sounded above their heads and Billy jumped to his feet. He stared up at the roof. 'You're right . . . it isn't a pigeon . . . it's another one of those *Dawn Demons*!'

16
No Smoke Without Fire

Strange sounds continued above their heads.

'Something's rolling down the roof,' Billy said, running over to the window. He stared through the glass and watched in disbelief as a large round potato dropped to the ground.

'It's a spud!'

More rumbling and rolling sounded above their heads. The three of them watched as another potato fell past the window.

'What the Devil's going on?' Henry stammered.

A *clunk* sounded from behind them. All three of them swung round and stared at the stove. The flames spit and hissed and turned to smoke.

'Something's fallen down the stove pipe and landed in the fire,' Calum said.

Before anyone had chance to react, a second *clunk* sounded, followed by a third and a fourth.

'I don't believe it! They're dropping potatoes down the chimney into the stove.'

As if to confirm the old man's theory, a fifth potato landed heavily in the fire and rolled out through the little glass door on to the floor. Smoke billowed into the room.

Billy charged out of the shed door, Calum close on his heels. He climbed up on to a water butt and stared up at the chimney. Calum clambered up beside him.

Their worst fears were confirmed!

One of the dolls was kneeling on the apex of the roof, its arms full of potatoes, stuffing them down the narrow chimney pipe. It glared down at them and spilt two of the potatoes . . . they rolled down the roof. Billy reached out and caught one. He drew his arm back and threw it with all his might at the doll. It missed.

The doll grinned an evil grin and turned its attentions towards them. They watched in horror as it climbed slowly to its feet. It stood perfectly balanced on the sloping roof and hurled a large potato with great strength. It struck Calum on the temple and knocked him off the water butt, flat on to the ground.

'Calum! Are you OK?' Billy shrieked, jumping down by his side.

Calum lay dazed on the muddy ground, the rain still

falling in torrents. 'Get . . . get . . . Henry out!' Calum stuttered. 'The smoke . . .!'

At first, Billy didn't understand what Calum was trying to say, but he turned round and saw that the shed was full of smoke. Then it clicked. The doll was blocking the chimney . . . filling it with potatoes . . . smoking the old man out!

Billy opened the door and saw Henry coughing and spluttering, trying desperately to put out the stove. But it was no good! The whole of the shed was filling rapidly with thick black smoke.

'GET OUT!' Billy screamed at him.

But the old man just dropped to his knees, gasping for breath. Without hesitation Billy raced in and grabbed hold of his arms. He pulled and pulled for all he was worth and dragged Henry towards the door and out into the rain.

Calum recovered and tried to help. 'The doll's still up there,' he said groggily. 'I can hear it moving about.'

Billy climbed back on to the water butt and watched open-mouthed as the doll bent back the chimney and squeezed it flat.

With the chimney sealed and completely blocked with potatoes, the stove began to overheat and belch flames into the shed. Once again, Calum was the first to realize the danger. 'GET BACK!' he screamed. 'IT'S GOING TO GO UP IN FLAMES!'

Billy jumped down and joined Henry, well away from the shed.

'All of you get back!' a voice shouted from behind them. 'I'll take over!'

They looked round and saw Bunty standing there in her shiny black plastic coat. She was wearing bright-pink Wellingtons patterned with yellow flowers.

'Bunty . . . you're back!' Billy cried out in surprise.

'What are you going to do?' Calum asked.

At first, Bunty didn't answer. She moved towards a pipe sticking up from the ground. It had a tap on the end and a length of hosepipe attached and coiled beneath it. 'I'm going to give our friend a little blast.'

Billy watched as Bunty turned on the tap and aimed a fierce jet of water towards the roof.

'You'll not put the fire out that way,' Henry shouted at her, trying to get back on his feet. 'You need to aim it inside.'

'I'm not trying to put the fire out,' Bunty retorted, climbing up on to the water butt. 'I'm going to wash away the pest on the roof.'

Billy and Calum jumped up beside her just in time to see the jet of water strike the doll on the side of the head. It immediately lost its balance, floundered and slipped down the far side of the roof and out of sight.

Bunty jumped down, still clinging on to the hosepipe. Billy and Calum did the same. They all jumped back as the shed began to go up in flames.

'Is it dead?' Calum asked, his voice full of hope.

'No way!' Bunty said. 'Like I told you, they're getting stronger. Stand behind me!'

They did as she said and waited, hearts beating faster, to see if the doll reappeared. More flames appeared through the shed window . . . the inside was beginning to turn into an inferno. At the same time, the rain began to ease . . . slowing to a drizzle . . . the light level increasing a little. But no sign of the doll!

'Where is it?' Calum asked.

'Gone back to join the others!' Billy suggested.

The clouds parted. The sun came out and dazzled them. Bunty lowered the water jet and shielded her eyes . . . just as the doll appeared from round the flaming shed and charged straight at her.

It was so intent on its target that it never saw Henry snatch up the old runner-bean net and throw it over its head. For all its strength the doll was rendered completely harmless. It struggled like a fish in a trawler net, biting and clawing at the mesh and screaming like a demented child.

'Brilliant!' Billy screamed.

Bunty said nothing. She scooped up the net, dragged it towards the burning shed and hurled it inside. She pulled the door closed and stepped back.

'NO!' Billy shrieked. 'Put out the fire . . . It's Henry's special place!'

The old man sauntered up and put his hand on Billy's shoulder. 'Leave it, son! Let it go! It's already ruined . . . due to that rat, Scullion. Let another piece of him go with it!'

They stood back and watched as the shed went up like matchwood and burnt to the ground. Within no time at all it was reduced to a pile of smoking rubble, an ominous black lump lying close to where the door had stood.

Billy looked up at Henry's sad, tear-filled eyes as he surveyed the smouldering remains. The last valuable thing in his life had gone. He grabbed the old man's arm and squeezed it. Calum did the same with Henry's other arm.

'We'll get rid of Scullion one way or another,' Billy said determinedly.

Henry looked down at them and forced a smile. 'The Three Musketeers, lad . . . that's what we are.'

Bunty walked over and joined them. She squeezed in between them and put her arms around Henry's waist. 'You mean, the Fabulous Four!' she said. 'Count me in!'

As they stood huddled together, the rain began to pour again. But they chose to remain there, clinging to each other, each of them sensing that together they made a formidable opposition for the evil power that stalked them.

A barking from nearby brought them back to reality.

They all watched in silence as the Alsatian bounded over and nuzzled up against Bunty's pink Wellingtons.

'That's settled then!' Bunty said with real determination in her voice. 'There's *five* of us! Scullion, here we come!'

A siren sounded somewhere in the distance.

'Are you OK?' a man shouted as he approached them. 'I saw the smoke and rang the fire brigade.'

'It's too late. My shed's already gone up,' Henry called back. 'But at least we're OK.'

They remained there, still in a group hug, relishing the moment, sensing their combined strength . . . waiting for the fire engine to arrive.

17 The Devil's Lair

An area of barren wasteland sprawled alongside the railway. Generations of weeds grew up the sides of the crumbling brickwork, hiding the old railway arches from public view.

One of the arches, more overgrown than the rest, still carried a familiar name stencilled in faded letters across its rusted metal doors.

SAMUEL SCULLION & Co.

Behind this barrier to the outside world, a large featureless room lay filled with stagnant air, its only occupants – rats – scurrying amongst the decaying wooden crates and other rubbish strewn across the damp stone floor.

To the rear of this dark chamber a door space led through into a winding passage. A ghostly high-pitched whispering sound echoed around its walls, coming from the direction of a shimmering light – from the festering office at the far end.

And in Scullion's former den, lit by a single candle, the two remaining Dawn Demons sat and waited, Scullion presiding over them, his intense evil power shared equally between them.

The hideous dolls grinned and sneered, one with jet-black hair, the other, blonde. Both with penetrating piggy eyes – twins of evil . . . twitching . . . restless . . . eager to strike.

And in this deepest, darkest place, Scullion's malicious spirit calculated and connived. He knew it would only be a matter of time before old Prior led the little gang of interfering brats into his lair. And his two remaining instruments of evil would be waiting – to kill them . . . to destroy the interfering mortal pests forever!

18
Henry Leads the Way

The sun had shone as the fire brigade doused the smouldering remains of Henry's allotment shed. The police had turned up and questioned them (Bunty and the dog had disappeared), but Henry remained disinterested and had not been very helpful. He'd mentioned the fact that he'd been a police officer, referred to one or two older colleagues – but no one knew them. This made Henry feel even more disinterested. 'Vandals!' was all he kept saying. 'You should find them . . . lock them up and throw away the key!'

The police had made a few notes and promised to look into it.

'Waste of time!' Henry had whispered to Billy and Calum. 'They'd never believe what really happened!'

And now they were back at Aunt Emily's, about to tuck into bangers and mash.

'It's the onion gravy that makes the meal really special,' Henry muttered. 'You can't beat it!'

Aunt Emily walked in and put their plates in front of them, stacked with creamy mashed potatoes and freshly-fried sausages. 'Right! I'll just get the gravy,' she said cheerily. 'I won't be a minute!'

Billy looked at Henry and smiled. He took the handcuffs from one of his trouser pockets and the key from the other. 'These are great,' he said. 'Look . . . I can do it. Hold your wrists out, Calum!'

Calum held his wrists above the table and Billy snapped the handcuffs around them in a matter of seconds.

'Not bad for a beginner,' Henry smiled. 'You've got to be even quicker than that when it's a real criminal. They might have a gun in their pocket.'

'Wow! I never thought of that,' Billy said.

'Whatever are you teaching them?' Aunt Emily said, carrying in the gravy boat. 'Why are Calum's wrists clamped? Is he on a diet?'

Henry smiled and Billy laughed out loud. He unlocked the cuffs and Calum began tucking into his meal. Aunt Emily went back to the kitchen.

The old man leant towards Billy and whispered, 'Tonight . . . you and Calum . . . are you up for it?'

'Up for what?' Billy asked quietly.

'Scullion's place! I know where it is. It's time we paid him a visit and put a stop to this business. If the police won't do it, then we'll see to it ourselves!'

Billy felt a nervous flutter in his stomach. Suddenly, the sausages and mashed potatoes didn't seem quite so appetizing.

Billy whispered Henry's intentions to Calum and asked him if he was up for it too. Calum looked even more nervous. 'I suppose so!' he replied. 'Do you think Bunty will turn up?'

Billy smiled to himself. It seemed that he wasn't the only one who felt safer when she was around. 'I hope so!' he whispered. He turned back to Henry. 'We're up for it! What time?'

'During the early hours . . . before dawn. I'll give you a knock. I never sleep much anyway.'

Billy smiled to himself again. He thought back to the loud snoring that they'd heard coming from the old man's room. 'OK, we'll be waiting. If we're asleep, just wake us up.' But Billy knew that there was no chance of either he or Calum getting much sleep – things were getting much too exciting.

Aunt Emily walked in with a large pot of tea and placed it on the table. 'Your mum's been on the phone, Billy. She wants you to give her a ring. She sounded a bit anxious. I told her you were fine, but Pauline always *was* a worrier.'

Billy and Calum looked at each other and frowned.

While Aunt Emily, Henry and Calum watched TV, Billy phoned his mum. She answered the phone straight away – as if she'd been waiting. 'Billy! Are you OK?'

Billy paused. 'Yes . . . why wouldn't I be?'

'Because something's going on! I can sense it!'

'It's Aunt Emily's lodger – Henry. His allotment shed's been burnt down by vandals!'

'It's more than that, Billy . . . Don't lie to me! I've been having strange dreams again. Terrible nightmares – some sort of dolls . . . horrible things! And I know that you're tied up in all this . . .'

Billy swallowed hard. He hated lying. But he wanted Mum and Aunt Emily well out of the way. 'Don't know what you're on about, Mum. Everything's fine. In fact, we've made friends with Henry – he's taking us out.' *Well at least that bit's true*, Billy thought to himself.

There was a long silence on the other end of the phone. Billy could almost see his mother taking a long puff on her cigarette. 'Are you sure, Billy? You would tell me, wouldn't you?'

'Sure, Mum.'

'I'll ring again tomorrow night.'

'OK, Mum – and stop worrying! Is Beth OK?'

'Yes, she's fine. But it's not her I'm worrying about. How's Calum getting on?'

Billy heard Calum laugh loudly from in the sitting room. Whatever he was watching on TV, it sounded really funny. 'He's fine, Mum. He's really enjoying it here. He loves Aunt Emily's meals.'

Billy's mum sounded more relaxed. 'Who wouldn't? Emily's a great cook. Give her my love and tell her I'll speak to her tomorrow evening. Now promise me that you'll take good care!'

'Promise, Mum.'

'Bye then.'

'Bye Mum . . . love you!'

'You too!'

Billy put the phone down and felt a lump in his throat. He hated not telling the truth, even when he knew it was for the best.

He walked back into the front room and sat next to Calum on the sofa. He took the handcuffs from his pocket and began playing with them. But Calum got tired of having his wrists clamped, so Billy sat on the rug and practised on Calum's ankles. Henry gave him a sly glance from his armchair. Billy looked at the clock on the mantelpiece: 9:30.

It wouldn't be too long before they were on their way to find Scullion's hiding place. Billy felt worried and excited at the same time. If Bunty and the dog turned up there would be five of them – brilliant! But what would be waiting when they got there?

* * *

Later, in bed, he and Calum went over everything that had happened again and again. They compared notes, compared ideas and even compared each other's feelings about the whole situation.

They finished up by admitting that they were both putting on a brave front. They were both extremely anxious about what the next twenty-four hours might hold for them.

But opening up and talking to each other was good – it made Billy feel a little more relaxed. Amazingly, he managed to fall asleep.

It was sometime during the early hours when he awoke to a sound from just outside the bedroom door.

Calum slept by his side, blissfully unaware.

Billy gripped the edge of the duvet and peered towards the door. He jumped at the sight of the soulful eyes staring in at him.

'Come on!' a familiar voice said in gruff tones. 'Don't make a noise. Emily's asleep.'

Billy woke Calum and the two of them slipped out of bed. They dressed silently while the old man waited patiently out on the landing. A few minutes later, Henry was leading them down the stairs with a powerful torch.

'The girl's waiting out in the street,' the old man whispered. 'I spotted her through my window. She's got the dog with her.'

'Brilliant!' Billy whispered back. Knowing Bunty was outside made him feel so much better. He suspected Calum felt the same.

A few seconds later, they were out in the street, greeting Bunty and the Alsatian. The night was clear and a full moon shone down from the starlit sky. But an ominous line of black clouds loomed on the horizon.

'I'll lead the way,' Henry commanded. He switched off the torch and put it in his pocket. 'Just keep your voices down and follow me . . . I know exactly where to go.'

'So do I!' Bunty chipped in. 'And it's my guess that they know we're on our way.'

'Who does?' Calum asked nervously.

'Scullion . . . and the dolls,' Bunty replied calmly. 'They'll be waiting.'

Billy felt his stomach tighten. 'How do you know?'

'Because she's a little mermaid and she knows everything!' Calum teased.

'Exactly!' Bunty giggled. 'You're learning!'

Henry moved forward and muttered over his shoulder. 'This is not the time for joking! Now keep quiet . . . and keep up.'

'OK, but keep the dog close – he'll spot danger before any of us,' Bunty said. She slid a length of rope around the dog's neck – it looked like an old skipping rope. The dog panted enthusiastically.

They moved off along the street.

There were lots of parked cars, otherwise Gladstone Terrace was completely deserted. But as they approached the end of the street, there was a definite movement around the corner. The dog growled.

'Get behind me!' Henry whispered. 'I'll go first.'

They edged along the privet hedge, Henry at the front, Bunty next, Billy and Calum taking up the rear.

As they turned into Belper Street, a tall figure staggered out in front of them. It was a scruffily-dressed man. He reeked of alcohol. 'Got any money?' He glowered at them.

'He's drunk,' Henry declared. 'Just ignore him and keep going!'

They sped on, the man shouting angrily after them, his curses ringing through the cold night air. The dog looked back and snarled.

'I hope we don't meet any more like him,' Calum said. 'He's definitely out of it.

Bunty smirked. 'He's the least of our problems.'

A short while later, Henry led them down the promenade. Everywhere seemed ghostly, bathed in shadows and completely devoid of people. The sea crashed on to the beach below, sounding ten times louder than during the day. Billy wondered if Uncle Jack was out there, his kindly spirit hovering over the inky-black waves.

The old man finally turned away from the seafront and led them away into an area unknown to Billy and Calum. Everywhere seemed run-down. The streets were narrower, darker and strewn with litter. Sounds of barking dogs and loud voices echoed from hidden alleyways and boarded-up houses.

'This is getting seriously scary,' Calum stammered.

'It gets worse,' Bunty said.

'How much further?' Billy asked.

Henry stared back at them. His big eyes somehow looked bigger at night. 'About five minutes – if we take the shortcut and nip down the snicket.'

'What's a snicket?' Calum asked.

'It's just a narrow passage between houses,' Henry replied.

'OK . . . let's go for it!' Billy said.

Bunty stopped. Her eyes sparkled under the streetlight. 'I think I know where he means. It's not a nice shortcut.'

'Why?' Billy and Calum whispered together.

'It's really dark and people hang out there . . . not very nice people!'

'It's called "Dead Man's Lane",' Henry said in his low gruff voice, 'We'll be fine – we'll just need to be on our guard.'

'It can't be any more dangerous than where we're heading,' Billy said.

'That's true,' Bunty replied. 'Come on! Keep moving!'

They crept on, stopping at every corner and constantly looking over their shoulder. The occasional car drove past . . . nothing unusual.

All the time, the Alsatian pulled at his rope, leading Henry on. But the dog suddenly stopped and the hackles on the back of his neck stood on end.

'Right, this is it,' Henry said. He crouched low and peered around the corner. Billy and Calum stared ahead.

A long narrow passage led off between the backs of two rows of houses. It was dimly lit and curved away into the distance – a perfect place for someone to wait in ambush!

'Blimey!' Calum muttered. 'Do we really have to go down there?'

' 'Fraid so!' Bunty replied, without a trace of nervousness in her voice.

'I'll stay at the front,' Henry said. 'Billy, you take up the rear.'

The dog gave a little whine and moved on – but this time much more slowly. Like mice being stalked by a cat, they set off down Dead Man's Lane, listening intently, wondering if anyone or anything might be waiting ahead of them.

The dog stopped suddenly and began to growl. They all stopped dead in their tracks and peered forward.

'Look, there's the end of the lane,' Bunty said in a low

voice. 'The Arches are just beyond, on the other side of that waste ground.'

As Billy and Calum looked to where she was pointing, two figures stood out in the distance. They faced each other, leaning against the high walls, blocking the exit to the lane. Even from far off, it was easy to make out the outline of the baseball caps!

'It's the Red Cap Gang, isn't it?' Calum stated rather than asked.

Bunty knelt down and peered forward. 'Yes, the gang you ran into the other day. They're bad news!'

'So what do we do now?' Calum asked nervously.

'We shift them!' Henry said, crouching down. 'Leave it to me!'

They watched as the old man took a mobile from his coat pocket and pushed the buttons. After a short pause, he whispered quickly into the phone.

'Hi, it's Prior here . . . ex-Detective Inspector Prior . . . the man you couldn't remember back on my allotment when my shed burnt down. Yes, that's me! Well, I've got something interesting for you. Two youths . . . drug dealing . . . end of Dead Man's Lane. They're there now . . . you'll catch them red-handed if you're quick.'

A smile spread across the old man's wrinkled features. 'OK, I'll wait. Hurry up or they'll be gone.'

Henry smiled again and put his phone back in his pocket. 'Now we wait!'

They all crouched in the shadows of the narrow lane and waited.

Sure enough, within five minutes a blue flashing light appeared on the scene. A scuffle broke out at the end of the lane as the two figures wearing baseball caps wrestled with three more figures.

'Got them!' Henry muttered loudly.

'Brilliant!' Billy said.

'Not quite!' Bunty pointed out. 'Look, that bigger guy is getting away.'

They watched with baited breath as the bigger of the two baseball-capped figures broke away and began sprinting up the dark passage – *straight towards them*.

The Alsatian jumped to his feet and began barking savagely.

They all tensed as the boy's shadow stopped about twenty yards away. With the police haring after him, the youth had no choice but to carry on towards them.

They watched in awe as he withdrew something ominous from one of his pockets – it was easy to make out what it was!

'Oh my God,' Calum cried. '*He's got a knife!*'

19
Ghost Attack

It was difficult to see exactly what was happening in the semi-darkness, but Billy was just able to make out Bunty pushing past Henry and hurling herself at the attacker. At the same time, the dog rushed forward snarling savagely.

'WATCH OUT!' Billy cried, as the knife struck down at Bunty. But she had already disappeared . . . vanished into thin air. They watched open-mouthed as the confused youth fell to the floor, the dog gripping his ankle in its tightly-clamped jaws. They retreated into the shadows as the police descended on him.

'You're nicked, mate!' they heard one of the policemen say.

Crouching in the darkness, no one spoke as the youth was dragged off, the dog still barking and being restrained by another policeman.

'Well done, boy!' the policeman kept saying.

Henry told them all to keep low whilst he went and had a word with the police. After another five minutes, the blue flashing lights had melted away into the night, the youths gone with them . . . Dead Man's Lane completely dead again. Henry made his way back to them.

'Brilliant, Henry!' Billy said.

'Yes, brilliant!' another voice said from somewhere behind them.

They jumped round and saw Bunty standing in the shadows.

'How did you disappear like that?' Billy asked in an incredulous voice.

'Because I'm a . . .'

'Little mermaid and you can do most things!' Calum finished for her.

'Wrong!' Bunty retorted. 'Because I'm a ghost – remember?'

'Keep quiet!' Henry ordered. 'We need to keep moving whilst the coast's clear. Where's the dog?'

They all looked round. The Alsatian had disappeared. 'He'll be back,' Bunty said. 'We're his friends. He'll not let us down.'

High above their heads, the clouds rolled in and the moon and stars disappeared. A breeze sprung up and it began to rain.

'That's all we need,' Calum complained, as they crept out from the end of the lane. They crossed the road and stood on the edge of a large expanse of waste ground.

'There they are – the Five Arches!' Henry pointed across the barren area to a huge road-bridge crossing the railway. The lines ran into an arched tunnel, but on either side, bordering the waste ground, a series of five smaller arches sprouted from the undergrowth.

'The arches used to be garages and workshops,' Henry whispered. 'They were abandoned years ago . . . That middle one is Scullion's old place.'

Calum was staring down at the ground. 'Look at these tracks!'

Henry took the torch from his pocket, switched it on and aimed the beam downwards. 'Motorbikes . . .' he said. 'They speed around here. They use it like a race track.'

Billy looked down at the tyre patterns rutted into the ground, 'Who does?'

'More bad guys!' Bunty whispered.

'Hell's blooming Angels for all I care!' Henry mumbled. 'Stop gassing and follow me!'

He shone his torch ahead and started across the waste ground towards the arches, Billy and the others following close behind.

An ominous roar sounded from somewhere over on their left.

'I don't believe it!' Bunty shrieked. 'The motorbikes – they're here!'

Everyone sped up, like insects running for cover. The rain fell faster and the ground became muddier. Henry slipped and fell heavily, twisting his ankle.

The roar became louder . . . more threatening. A light shone out in the distance . . . and then two lights . . . becoming larger and brighter with every passing second.

'We need to get out of here!' Calum cried desperately.

'I've twisted my damn ankle,' Henry uttered.

Billy and Bunty helped Henry back to his feet as the two huge machines sped towards them.

'Do you think they've seen us?' Billy asked.

'They've seen us all right!' Henry stammered. He reached down and picked up his torch – it was still lit. 'They've seen this!' He switched it off.

'Give me the torch,' Bunty shrieked. 'I'll sort them out!'

'What are you going to do?' Billy asked.

'You'll see.'

They watched in wonder as Bunty ran some distance away and switched on the torch. The leading bike turned and headed towards it, homing in on the light like a moth to a candle flame.

'What's she doing?' Calum whispered.

'Trust her!' Billy replied.

'I'm not so sure, lad!' Henry muttered. 'I'm not so sure!'

Bunty shone the powerful beam straight at the approaching motorcycle. It accelerated towards her . . . but she never moved!

Billy could hardly bring himself to watch. 'It's going to smack straight into her!'

But as the lethal machine bore down on her, the only collision was between one very confused motor- cyclist and a rubber torch. The bike skidded on the muddy ground and crunched on to its side, the rider screaming beneath it. They watched as the toppled machine slid to a halt. The second biker roared over and pulled up beside it.

'You OK, mate?' they heard him shout.

The bruised rider replied with a string of swear words, his curses ringing through the damp night air.

'Serves him right!' Billy chuckled.

Even Henry cheered up at the spectacle. 'That Bunty's a gutsy lass.'

'Glad you think so!' Bunty whispered, sneaking up from behind.

'I wish you'd stop doing that!' Calum said, his voice trembling.

'Sorry!' Bunty said softly. 'Look who's back!'

As the two motorcycles cruised slowly away, they turned and saw that the dog was back by Bunty's side.

'Good boy!' Billy said, affectionately patting the dog's head. 'We're five again!'

'He disappears almost as much as you do,' Calum said to Bunty in a teasing sort of way.

'That's because we're two of a kind,' Bunty said, crouching down and stroking the Alsatian's head. 'He's beautiful, aren't you baby?'

Henry was too busy looking ahead to take any notice. 'We need to get the torch back . . . and then let's get off this open space before they come back.'

'Leave it to us!' Bunty said. She whispered in the dog's ear and he set off towards where she was pointing. It returned a minute later with the torch in its mouth – it was still lit.

'Good boy!' Henry said, taking the torch from the dog and hurriedly turning it off.

They finally moved on across the waste ground and arrived by an overgrown archway. Through the clinging weed-like vegetation, Billy read the faded letters stencilled across the rusted metal doors:

SAMUEL SCULLION & Co.

'That's the way in,' Bunty whispered. She pointed to a gap between the rusted metal door and the stonework.

'It looks a bit tight,' Calum said.

'Just big enough for you know what to get in and out!' Bunty said.

'Those damn dolls!' Henry stammered.

Billy scanned around. No one in sight! He swallowed hard. 'Can we squeeze through?'

'And what about Henry?' Calum joined in. 'He's far too big.'

'It's OK, son!' Henry groaned. 'My ankle's done for. I think I've sprained it. You'll have to go in there without me. Here . . . take this!' He passed Billy a small haversack. 'There's a few things in there that might come in handy.'

Billy looked inside . . . matches, a candle and some rolled-up netting. 'Thanks! Are you sure you'll be OK?'

'I'll be fine. In any case, I can keep watch. If I need to, I can use this.' He held up his mobile.

'OK! Let's go!' Billy said with as much confidence as he could muster.

'Right!' Bunty said. 'It looks like we're back to four again!'

The dog ran up to the gap and sniffed at it. His fur stood on end and he began to whine.

'That's what he thinks about going in there!' Calum said.

To make the point, the dog tucked his tail between his legs and slouched away.

'OK, wrong again . . . We're the Three Musketeers!' Bunty said with a half-smile. 'We'll manage.'

The bank of black cloud moved across the moon and it grew darker overhead; the rain began to fall faster . . .

Henry groaned and rubbed his ankle – he looked tired and cold.

Things had not gone well . . . and the worst was probably still to come.

Billy and Calum watched as Bunty strode over to the door where the gap was. It was the only part of the arch not overgrown with weeds . . . *because it's still in use*, Billy thought to himself.

Bunty got down on to all-fours and pulled on the metal; the gap widened. 'OK, let's get in there!' she said determinedly. 'I'll go first.'

Billy watched, half in admiration, half in horror as she crawled through the tight space. 'Come on then!' she called from the other side. 'Bring the torch.'

'OK, Billy . . . let's go for it!' Calum whispered in his ear.

Billy nodded. He took the torch from Henry, got down on to all-fours and crawled towards Bunty's shadowy face. A shiver ran down his spine as he heard a sinister scurrying from somewhere in the blackness behind her.

So this is it, he thought to himself, *the last of the Dawn Demons*.

20
Lair of the Dawn Demons

The three friends found themselves inside a large vaulted room. It was damp and smelt fusty, like the inside of a derelict house.

They crouched by the door and Billy scanned around with the torch.

It was an enormous untidy storage space. Lots of wooden crates were scattered around. Shelves, many of them collapsed, were stacked with rusty tins. Cardboard boxes lay on the floor, covered in mould, misshapen, everything in a state of neglect and decay.

'I can't see anybody, can you?' Billy asked, his voice quaking slightly.

'No!' Bunty whispered. 'Let's move on. There's some sort of door space on the far wall.'

As Billy and Calum followed Bunty, something small

scurried between two crates in the distance.

Billy's heart began to beat faster. 'Did you see that?'

'Yes,' Bunty whispered. 'I think it was one of them!'

Billy tensed and clenched his fists. 'Shall we go on?'

'Yes,' Bunty murmured in a low voice. 'Just stick together.'

They passed close to some dirty wooden crates stacked on a pallet. The labels had long since faded or dropped off.

Billy saw that one of the boxes had the lid hanging off. He couldn't resist standing up and peering into the top. His heart almost stopped when he saw the contents: painted dolls' heads – sailor dolls' heads, their beady eyes staring up at him . . . lifeless, but sinister!

'What is it?' Bunty asked in a hushed tone.

'Body parts . . . for Dawn Demons!'

Bunty winced and pulled a face. 'Let's go . . . keep moving!'

They crept on, Billy growing more nervous by the second, sure that something was hiding in front of them, waiting to jump out!'

Now only one row of crates stood between them and the door space.

'I'm sure there's something hiding just in front of us,' Billy whispered.

Bunty pressed up close by his side. 'You're right! Listen . . . I can hear it moving.'

Billy listened. He listened so hard he could hear his own heartbeat. Bunty was right . . . there *was* something moving up ahead.

'What shall we do?' Calum asked nervously from behind.

Billy clenched his fists again. 'I'm going to have to face it.'

Bunty picked up a length of wood from the floor. 'We'll face it together.'

'Don't forget me!' Calum whispered. Bunty picked up another piece of wood and passed it back to him.

The three of them took a deep breath and leapt around the side of the crate. A shrill scream echoed around the empty space as a tatty-looking cat jumped into the air. It hissed and spat at them, before running off and disappearing underneath a pile of rubbish.

'God!' Billy gasped. 'I've never been so glad to see an old moggy!'

'Me too!' Bunty sighed.

Calum said nothing. He was still shocked and speechless.

They headed on towards the dark door space in the corner. As they approached, Bunty stopped in her tracks. 'I can hear something else.'

They crouched and listened.

Billy felt his heart turn to ice as a horrific high-pitched giggling sounded from somewhere beyond.

'They're down there!' Calum said, his voice shaking. 'Now what?'

'We face them!' Bunty said. 'Come on!'

They followed her through the door space. She shone the torch ahead, lighting up a creepy winding passage. The torch beam sent numerous spiders shooting back up their webs and a rat scurried away into a dark corner.

'Do we have to go down there?' Calum asked, clutching his wooden weapon.

The horrible giggling sounded again, distant and menacing. Billy agreed . . . The prospect of going down the spooky passage did not seem a nice one.

Bunty tried to reassure them. 'We'll be fine . . . just stay close,' she said, raising her piece of wood.

They crept slowly on . . . A faint light flickering in the distance. The giggling stopped and all went silent. Billy was sure he could hear Calum's heart beating behind him – or was it his own?

A hollow-sounding voice screeched from behind them.

'*Three blind mice, three blind mice . . . see how they run!*'

The three friends swung round and Bunty's torch lit up the face of the demonic figure. It was standing about ten metres behind, back at the door space. A Dawn Demon, wielding a baseball bat and glowering at them. Long strands of jet-black hair stuck out from the sailor cap slung carelessly on its head. Thick painted eyebrows angled over its eyes gave it an expression of devilish purpose.

'*It spoke!*' Billy said, not sure what else to say.

'Doesn't surprise me! It's like I told you – these last two are more powerful than the others,' Bunty whispered. 'There's no telling what they can do.'

'OK! What now?' Billy whispered.

But before anyone had a chance to reply, the doll screamed a high-pitched scream and charged straight at them.

Bunty didn't hesitate. She ran to meet it and brought her weapon crashing down on its head. It never flinched . . . just kept on running. It ran straight through Bunty, lunged at Billy and struck his right knee heavily with the bat. As Billy screamed and fell to the floor, the doll swung another blow and struck Calum in the stomach, sending him reeling back into the wall. The attacker shrieked in glee and ran on, disappearing around the bend of the passage.

As Billy and Calum groaned and tried to scramble back to their feet, Bunty reappeared from the shadows. She bent down to examine the torch where Billy had dropped it–it laid smashed on the stone floor.

'What hit me?' Calum groaned.

Billy rubbed his knee frantically, trying to ease the pain. 'They're too strong for us!' he sighed. 'But we can't give up now. We need a plan.'

'Well try and think of something,' Bunty whispered in a determined tone of voice. 'And quick!'

Billy slid down on to the floor, his back up against the cold stone wall. He tried to forget the pain in his knee and concentrate on the haversack that Henry had given him. He rummaged in the bag, took out the candle and matches, lit the candle and looked deeper into its contents . . . saw the netting.

'OK! Sit with your backs to the wall, like I'm doing . . . you on one side and Calum on the other. Hurry!'

Calum was only too happy to sit down. He was still winded from the blow on his stomach. Bunty sat opposite him, the soles of her plimsolls pressed up firmly against the soles of his trainers.

'Now what do we do?' Bunty asked. She sounded as if she was enjoying herself.

'Hold this netting between you and keep it tight,' Billy ordered. He held the candle in one hand and rolled out the netting on the floor with the other. He passed one end to Calum and the other to Bunty.

Bunty pulled tightly on the netting. Calum pulled back hard on his side. The net stretched out upright between them, like a small tennis net.

'Now what do we do?'

'Wait!' Billy said, walking away from them. He walked back up the passage, back towards the door space, leaving Bunty and Calum hidden in the shadows.

The net wasn't visible at all. 'Hold that net really tight,' he whispered.

He stood in the middle of the passage, took a deep breath, and shouted at the top of his voice. 'COME OUT AND FIGHT! WE'RE READY AND WAITING! WE'RE NOT SCARED! YOU'RE JUST DOLLS – SILLY LITTLE SAILOR DOLLS – CONTROLLED BY A CROOK . . . A COWARD . . . SCULLION!'

Billy's challenge echoed down the passage and faded away. All went deathly silent. Bunty and Calum sat like stone statues and held the net tight. Billy couldn't even hear them breathing. He stretched out his arm, holding the candle high; half expecting to see something creeping into view – but there was still nothing.

'SO YOU'RE SCARED . . . YOU'RE NOT DAWN DEMONS, YOU'RE JUST FAIRY DOLLS. YOU SHOULD BE ON THE TOP OF A CHRISTMAS –'

Billy never had chance to finish. A high-pitched scream rang through the corridor as the Dawn Demon charged. Even in the shadowy darkness, Billy could see that it was still holding the baseball bat poised high above its head.

As the doll came into view, the candle lit up its face, enhancing its demonic features. Its head stood out and glowed like some sort of ghastly hologram. It hit the net and crashed to the floor, the baseball bat rattling across the ground and arriving at Billy's feet. Bunty and Calum tried desperately to wrap the net around the creature, but it was too strong. It bit and clawed and tore the net apart, springing back to its feet.

And that's when Billy brought the bat down with incredible determination, and knocked its head clean off its shoulders.

Everyone winced as the grotesque wooden head clattered down the passage, still shrieking and screaming. The wriggling body fell back on to the netting and Bunty jumped on it, sitting on it and wrapping it up at the same time. With its head separated from its shoulders, the doll had no sense of direction . . . It quickly lost its strength and the wooden body lapsed into stillness. The head rolled to a standstill and went silent, staring up at the roof of the passage with painted lifeless eyes.

'Wow . . . you've done it again, Billy!' Calum shrieked.

Billy walked down the passage and held his candle over the doll's head. He gazed down triumphantly at the useless lump of wood.

'One to go!' he said, almost to himself.

Bunty walked up to him. 'But twice as strong!' she said. 'This time we'll be up against all of Scullion's power – the whole caboodle!'

Calum trotted up to them. 'You mean the full Monty!'

'*Call me what you will!*' A hideous voice sounded from somewhere down the creepy passage.

The three friends edged around the bend of the creepy corridor and gasped at the sight of the silhouette standing in the candlelit doorway at the end of the passage.

It was the last remaining Dawn Demon – *twice as big as any of the others*, about the same size as Billy – and wearing a white sailor suit.

'Whoaah!' Calum whined. 'It's massive!'

'It's only as big as us!' Bunty said, clenching her fists.

Billy glanced from the devilish fiend standing before them to Bunty's face, full of grim determination.

Uncle Jack had been right. Her desire for revenge had been a danger to him – and to Calum. Along with Henry, she had brought them here – to face this evil of all evils. It was her battle, not theirs!

And then Billy thought of Bunty's mum and how Scullion had taken everything from her . . . Made her so desperate that she'd walked off the end of the pier – taking her own life as well as her daughter's. And then his mind flashed to old Henry, sitting outside in the cold and wet, nursing his sprained ankle, his house burnt down and his allotment hut in ruins. And he thought of Aunt Emily and how her garden had been wrecked – Aunt Emily, who would never hurt anyone.

Still clutching the candle in his right hand, he clenched his left fist as the anger welled up inside him. He stared ahead at the sinister figure, still standing in the doorway at the end of the passage. He braced himself, sure the doll would charge.

'OK,' Billy yelled at the top of his voice. 'LET'S FINISH THIS JOB . . . WHO'S WITH ME?'

'Count me in!' Bunty shrieked.

'Me too!' Calum cried.

But the Dawn Demon just stood there, leaning casually against the door frame. It folded its arms and began to laugh hysterically. It was a laugh guaranteed to send shivers down the spine, cover the skin in goosebumps, make the hairs on the back of the neck stand on end.

The three friends took a deep breath and stepped forward – nobody sure what to do, but determined to face up to the last of the Dawn Demons.

But the doll just turned, walked into the room and slammed the door.

21
Battle of Wits

It was Bunty who got to the door first. Without hesitation, she pushed it open and Billy and Calum followed her inside.

The big doll sat back in a swivel chair and glared at them over a large desk strewn with musty papers.

'Come in, why don't you?' it squawked in a grating high-pitched voice.

Billy looked nervously at the creepy face. Unlike any of the previous dolls, this one had straggly straw-blonde hair. It's eyes seemed even more penetrating and its expression altogether more threatening.

'So you *can* speak!' Billy said.

'Shut up!' the doll snapped back. It leant back in the chair and put its hands behind its head. 'I could kill you all!'

Billy was shocked at the brutal manner in which the doll spoke. His stomach began to churn as Bunty stepped forward. 'I'm already dead, you stinking creep . . . thanks to Scullion. You're just a lump of wood!' she said, her voice trembling with emotion.

The hideous figure slapped its wooden hands on the desk and a cloud of dust rose into the fusty air. It began to giggle hysterically. 'I *am* Scullion!' the doll shrieked. 'This is me . . . inside this "useless lump of wood", as you call it – bigger than the other dolls because I was going to display it in the entrance to the biggest, glitziest arcade in the town. But it never happened . . . thanks to Detective Inspector Prior.'

'And we'll destroy you like all the other dolls,' Calum said bravely.

The Scullion doll paused, stood up and stared across at Calum with an expression of pure evil. 'I could jump across this desk and snap your neck in a second.'

The three friends tensed, stepped back and braced themselves.

Calum's voice trembled slightly. 'No way!'

'We're together!' Bunty said defiantly. 'All for one and one for all.'

'Like the Three Musketeers!' Billy added.

Turning to face him, the Scullion doll scowled and giggled at the same time. 'Billy Hardacre! You interfering brat!'

Billy stared back and saw the fuzzy image of Scullion's face superimposed over that of the doll. He wasn't sure whether it was real, or in his mind, but the fat round face, piggy eyes and thick scowling lips became clearer by the second.

'I'm the one who really caused you trouble,' Bunty snapped angrily. 'Billy just got involved . . . came along for the ride.'

The doll turned its spooky head towards Bunty. 'I can't kill you – you're already dead, like your useless mother.'

Bunty's face puffed up and her eyes blazed with anger. 'Exactly!' she said, raising her weapon. 'And it was you that killed her.'

'Don't flatter me! She killed herself! I did her a favour. I loaned her money. She only had to pay back what she owed . . . plus a little extra for my trouble.'

Bunty raised her weapon even higher. 'Plus a whole lot extra. You took everything . . . left us with nothing. We had nowhere to live. We couldn't even afford to eat. And in the end Mum was so desperate she decided the only way out was for us both to die.'

The Scullion doll shrieked with laughter. 'Do you really think I care?'

Bunty leapt forward and brought the stout piece of wood down towards the doll's head. But the Scullion doll was not only bigger, it was quicker than the others.

It caught hold of Bunty's weapon, wrenched it out of her hand and snapped it like a flimsy twig. Bunty jumped back, shocked at the doll's lightning reaction.

'Enough!' the Scullion doll screeched. 'It's time to put an end to all this. I'm sick and tired of interfering brats, old men, and stinking run-down seaside towns . . .'

'So what are you going to do?' Bunty hissed.

The doll glared across at Billy. 'You should never have come here! You've mucked up my plans – you and your pal. I think it's time you were taught a lesson!'

The Scullion doll leapt over the desk and pinned Billy to the wall. 'Ahh, poor little boy! I'm going to squeeze the life out of you. And then you and Bunty can be together forever!'

Billy gasped and pushed at the doll's face. It wouldn't budge. It held him in a vice-like grip and stared him straight in the eye. Billy screamed at his two friends, 'GERRITOFF!'

Bunty pulled frantically at the doll's neck. Calum did the same. The Scullion doll shrieked and giggled hysterically. It pushed against Billy so hard he could hardly breathe. 'Say goodbye, Billy-boy!'

Calum wrestled an ancient-looking fire extinguisher off the wall. He tried to pull out the pin and release the lever, but it wouldn't budge . . . it was too rusted.

'Give it here!' Bunty shrieked.

As Billy struggled to breathe, Bunty snatched the

heavy metal extinguisher from Calum and brought it down heavily on the back of the doll's head. *CLANG!*

The Scullion doll released its grip momentarily and Billy managed to wrestle himself free.

'Run for it!' Bunty shrieked. 'It can't kill me . . . You and Calum get out of here!'

Billy slid along the wall and leapt out of the door, Calum hot on his heels. The two friends ran out into the blackness of the winding passage. Billy's candle had long since disappeared.

'It's me he's after!' Billy yelled, sensing Calum's presence, close behind.

But Calum never answered. The Scullion doll had already caught up with him. It punched him heavily in the back and knocked him to the ground . . . clambered over him . . . screamed after Billy.

Billy ran on, trusting his instincts to lead him back to the entrance, all the time the last of the Dawn Demons shrieking behind . . . closing in on him.

He reached the door space at the top of the passage and leapt through into the vaulted chamber. 'I've got to get outside . . . think of something,' Billy said to himself.

'I'm closing on you, Billy-boy!' the doll shrieked from behind. 'Nearly time for bye-byes!'

Billy ignored the taunting voice. 'He sprinted on harder and his heart filled with hope at the sight of the heavy metal doors and the gap where they'd crept in.

'I'm still here, Billy!' the voice giggled behind him.

He pulled heavily on the corner of the door and thrust himself through the gap – but the doll gripped his left foot and stopped him. With his head sticking through into the cold night air, he looked around frantically and saw Henry still sitting there with the dog by his side. 'HELP!' Billy yelled. 'GET ME OUT!'

'Good grief!' Henry yelled back.

The dog ran over and licked Billy's nose. Henry grabbed Billy's arms and began to pull for all he was worth. At the same time, the Dawn Demon pulled so hard on his foot it felt as if his ankle was about to break.

Billy felt his trainer loosen. Thankfully, his lace wasn't tied very well and, as the Scullion doll pulled even harder, his trainer came off. He slid through the gap and out into the cold air.

'What's going on?' Henry croaked. 'Is everyone OK?'

'It's behind me! Keep back and phone the police!' Billy yelled at the old man.

He scrambled to his feet and ran on, towards the edge of the waste ground, not sure where he was going or what to do, but sure that the Scullion doll would still be on his tail. Maybe the Alsatian would attack it and slow it down.

He was right. As he ran along the fence bordering the railway embankment, he heard the dog barking frantically from somewhere behind. And then a pitiful series of yelps told Billy that his pursuer had got the upper hand. The Dawn Demon closed in again.

'YOU CAN'T ESCAPE ME, BILLY . . . I'M GOING TO KILL YOU!' . . . STOP YOU INTERFERRING THEN SHE'LL HAVE NO ONE TO HELP HER!

Billy's heart felt as if it was about to burst. He saw a gap between the iron railings and a plan formed in his mind. He plunged through the gap and hurtled down the steep railway embankment. Seconds later he was running along the edge of the railway lines, the shrieking sailor only fifty or so metres behind.

Billy looked up the line – no trains. He glanced behind – no trains – just his pursuer closing the gap between them. He sank to his knees and braced himself for the attack. He looked up the line again – and thought he saw a distant light!

Yes! A train! he thought to himself. *I've got to keep running*.

With renewed hope, he leapt to his feet and ran on towards the approaching train. But with every step his legs turned more and more to jelly. He had no more energy.

'THIS IS IT, BILLY-BOY!' the voice sounded from behind. 'YOU'RE ALL MINE!'

The horrific figure jumped on to Billy's back, knocked him to the ground and pinned him to the rails. It sat astride his chest and leered down at his face.

'You're dead meat, Billy-boy . . . about to join that friend of yours, Bunty . . . become a stupid ghost, just like her and her mother . . . walk in paradise forever – and all that crap . . . ha ha ha . . .'

Billy gazed upwards, past the doll's face, to the sky. Towards the horizon he could see that it was blood-red. Uncle Jack's words rang through his mind: '*Red sky dawning . . . sailor's warning!*'

This is it! Billy thought to himself. *Uncle Jack tried to warn me . . . the final showdown.*

The super-strong doll gurgled and giggled, revelling in Billy's helplessness. It was so intent on his demise that it never saw the train in the distance. It wrapped its heavy wooden hands around Billy's neck and began to squeeze.

Billy tried desperately to slide his left hand into his pocket. But it was no good. The doll was too strong. As it squeezed tighter, he felt the faintness coming over him. *This is it . . . the end!*

The train sounded a loud whistle, and for the first time the doll looked up and saw it. It instinctively released its grip on Billy – just for a few seconds, but time enough . . .

Billy plunged his hand into his pocket and felt the coldness of the shiny metal.

At lightning speed, he withdrew the handcuffs, snapped one half around the doll's wrist, the other on to the rails.

The Scullion doll hardly had time to work out what had happened. It stared bewilderedly at the stainless-steel band around its wrist. At the same time it looked up again at the approaching train. 'What the . . . ?'

Billy wriggled and tried to free himself, but he was trapped firmly under the doll's weight. The Scullion doll pulled, and pulled but the handcuffs held it fast – like an animal snared in a trap. It shrieked and screamed into the cold dewy air, the train looming ever closer.

Billy lay there, the noise of the diesel engine filling his ears. *This is the end*, he thought to himself, *but at least Scullion will go with me*. But then the doll pulled so hard it wrenched its arm clean out of its socket. It jumped to its feet, put one foot on Billy's chest and glowered down at him. 'Nice try, Billy,' the gruesome figure grinned. 'It was nice knowing you . . . I don't think!'

The train was only seconds away. Billy tried to roll off the line but the doll's heavy foot held him firm. It was so strong he couldn't move a muscle. This was surely the end!

'Like I said, Billy . . . bye-bye!'

'AND "BYE-BYE" TO YOU TOO!' a familiar voice yelled, only just audible above the noise of the approaching train.

All in a blur, Billy looked up and saw Bunty clinging to the doll's back, her arms around its neck, her hands covering its eyes. 'Guess who?' she taunted.

With only a second to spare, the doll stumbled backwards down the line with Bunty still clinging on in true piggyback style. It screamed its curses and tried to shrug Bunty off. But she held on with all her strength.

Freed from the doll's heavy foot, Billy instinctively rolled himself off the rails. The train arrived at almost the same instant. He clenched his teeth as the train ploughed into the wooden sailor, the roaring of the diesel engine drowning out its screeching cries. He looked over his shoulder as another figure scrambled down the embankment towards him. 'Are you OK? What happened?' Calum shrieked.

Billy looked back to the railway lines, to the spot where the last of the Dawn Demons had met its fate. An ominous ring of black mist hovered above the rails. He climbed slowly to his feet and Calum joined him. The two of them watched in awe as the cloud began to change and distort. Billy thought he could see Scullion's evil features in it . . . fat piggy face . . . scowling through thick leathery lips.

'What *is* that?' Calum whispered to Billy.

'It's Scullion's spirit!' Billy replied. 'Or at least, what's left of it!'

They continued to stare as Bunty materialized in the ghostly mist . . . and then two other spectral figures joined her. Billy recognized one of them as Uncle Jack.

'What's going on?' Calum asked.

The dog stayed close to Billy's legs, whining and winging, all its fur standing on end.

'Scullion's victims . . .' Billy said knowingly. 'They're joining forces.

'I can't see anyone,' Calum said frustratingly.

It seemed that Calum could only see the ring of black mist. But Billy watched in fascination as the three ghostly figures linked hands and stood in a circle beneath the black cloud. The figures glowed . . . brighter and brighter . . . until they formed a glowing ring so bright that Billy had to shield his eyes.

'What's happening now?' Calum gasped. 'What can you see?'

'They're stronger than him,' Billy said, 'the three spirits – Uncle Jack, Bunty . . . and her mother. They're forcing him back . . . to where he belongs . . .'

Calum nodded. They watched the black cloud begin to fade and break up . . . finally disappearing altogether.

And then Billy watched the three figures walk off into the distance and fade in the same way.

The two friends stood in silence. They walked towards the railway line, to the post where the black cloud had hovered . . . nothing to see, like it had all been a dream.

Henry appeared from somewhere in the distance, limping badly. 'Are you all right, lad?' he asked. 'What happened here?'

Billy turned away from Henry's worried expression

back to the railway lines. He saw in his mind's eye the remnants of the doll being ground to dust . . . all traces of the last remaining Dawn Demon gone forever.

'It's over,' he said. 'Scullion's gone and Bunty's gone. She rescued me, gave her life – except she was dead already, I suppose. There's only the dog left.'

The Alsatian licked his hand. *The Three Musketeers, Bunty would have said*, Billy thought to himself. He felt a lump form in his throat. He tried to explain to Henry what had happened. But it was all too much to take in.

'Come on,' Henry said. 'Let's get home. 'You can tell me later.'

The old man struggled the short distance to the station, the two boys taking it in turns to support his weight – his ankle had swollen badly. The dog went with them. Henry muttered something about keeping it . . . good company for him . . . a trusted friend and all that.

From the station, they took a taxi. It was a clever idea; as far as the driver was concerned, the three of them had just returned on the night train and needed a lift home.

But when they did finally get home, Aunt Emily was up and waiting for them. And as she quite rightly said – *they had some explaining to do*!

Epilogue

The following day, the weather was glorious.

With as much sorted out as could be sorted out, Billy's mum had returned to take the boys home, and they were all sitting on the seafront. Billy's mum and Aunt Emily were sipping tea on the promenade. Billy, Calum and Beth were sitting down on the beach in sight of them.

Calum looked out over the flat calm sea. Billy played with Beth, digging in the sand. 'Look, Billy!' Calum suddenly said. 'There's boat out there. I think it's the lifeboat . . . It must be on a practice run.'

Billy gazed out to where Calum was pointing. At first he couldn't see anything. And then he saw the small vessel – a faint glimmer of orange and blue – a good way out to sea. 'Yes, I can see it,' he said enthusiastically. 'I couldn't see it at first . . . Those people paddling – the girl and her mum – they were in the way.'

Calum looked puzzled. 'What people? I can't see anyone paddling!'

Billy got up and sauntered down to the shoreline. He peered out over the small waves to the girl and saw that she was standing on the surface of the water. She waved at him and a familiar voice sounded softly in his head: '*Thanks for everything, Billy! We did it – the Three Musketeers. Say Hi to Calum . . . Take care!*'

He stumbled further into the sea – he couldn't help it. He waved back at her. 'Bunty! Bunty! Don't go!'

'Billy! Are you OK?' a voice shouted from behind.

Billy looked back. Calum was staring at him in a strange way. Beth had stopped digging; she looked concerned.

He struggled for words . . . turned back to the sea and pointed . . . but she was gone.

This time he knew that Bunty was gone forever. He turned back and waved to Calum . . . waved to Beth . . . went back to his place on the beach.

'Come on, Billy!' Calum said. 'It's my turn to buy the ice creams.'

Billy smiled and nodded his head. 'Brilliant!'